2000 DECIDUOUS TREES

Memories of a Zine

By NATH JONES

LIFE LIST PRESS

CHICAGO · 2011

Life List Press
Chicago, IL

PUBLISHER'S NOTE

These selections are works of fiction. Names, characters, places, and incidents are either the product of the author's imagination or are used fictionally and any resemblance to actual persons, living or dead, business establishments, events, or locales is entirely coincidental

ISBN-10: 1937316130
ISBN-13: 978-1-937316-13-6

Book design by Gin Y. Havard
Author photo by Louisa Podlich
Cover image by Yulia Drozdova

Printed in the United States of America

For Chris

TABLE OF CONTENTS

INTRODUCTION

There were only four issues of *The Skirt*—one of those reality-bite kinds of zines—before 9/11, which, for me, changed everything about the grungy apathy and artistic incapacity of the 1990s when we had endless potential and the freedom to do absolutely nothing with it.

We were a generation on couches. We had a fuck-all attitude and considered this a luxury. We wrote what we wanted and stapled it together for friends.

Of all the moments of Scotch tape, scissors, darkroom chemicals, cardstock, sketches, fonts, stacks of paper on the carpet, heavy-duty staplers, cool pens, trips to the copy shop, coffee, and collages, my favorite production memory is of my boyfriend taping the black duct tape bindings of that first hot pink issue. He was so precise about something bound to be informal.

Hundreds of copies of *The Skirt* were mailed from my little apartment at Purdue. The zine was sprinkled everywhere: Chicago, Madison, Indianapolis, Austin, Grand Rapids, Lancaster, Alameda, Poughkeepsie, San Antonio, Boston, Santa

Fe, Brooklyn, Rochester, Denver, Athens, Springfield, and to the guy upstairs.

Issues of *The Skirt* went to a friend stationed on a military installation in Korea and also sat in a Sarasota hospital waiting room between checkups when another friend was having her finger reattached.

The Skirt was the subject of academic discussion in Poland and was read with late-night laughing cigarettes by the cool kids in New Orleans. A friend teaching physics for the Peace Corps received issue number 4 in Kenya while another copy traveled across thirteen time zones with a dear friend who told me in a letter, "I went to a native island in Indonesia where all the natives wear loincloths, etc. I missed a perfect chance to get a picture of them reading (er *looking at*) *The Skirt*."

It's strange to look back at this writing. The maw of one's twenties is frightful. But I've left most of the pieces intact with all the embarrassing vigor and hope of their careless origins.

ANY PILE OF WOOD

Alone isn't one day of sitting on a rock exactly the right size for you. It isn't the deep furrow in your father's brow. It isn't Mother's giving-up and watching the window eternally. It isn't the neglect of the community or a lack of friends.

It's a force, an emotion, like love. It's wanting someone to come in the door when you're naked. It's talking to a dinner guest who wasn't ever invited. It's noticing that the grout between the tiles in the bathroom is black and taking the time to paint it deep forest green.

It's crying when you see a mannequin being dressed in a storefront window. It's endlessly arranging the furniture in your mind without the strength to move your arm or your feet or your back to move the couch or the bed or the furnace or the recliner. It's waiting for the phone to ring and pretending that's what you wanted. It's throwing yourself at an illusion. It's nothing. Nothing but you. And that can mean anything at all.

Alone is petrification in the bed in the morning, finally giving up inhibition, imagining what the cat feels as the whiskers escape slowly from her head, or wondering what the dog's collar might feel like, choking on your own happy leash-length run.

It's showering with a mirror between your legs. It's building an altar over the sink. It's asking that the clothes you buy for yourself be gift-wrapped. It's patience. It's a beer belly. It's strong lean muscles. It's repetition and it's divorced from reality. It's faith, a religion of constant prayer. It's worshiping beauty without pursuit. It's learning. It's understanding the world and falling through reason over yourself.

It's memory with or without regret. It's pain.

Alone discourages living in the present. It is dreaming of an unattainable future and it's a consumption by a hole somewhere inescapable but often postponed. It is the electric bill and late-night television. It's *Jesus, I guess I have to* and calling that other fool from work. It's compromise. It's knowing your body and fearing the mind's retreat. It's nothing to be fooled around with. *Alone* is the impossibility of fire as much as any pile of wood and a wet match.

It's the soul's house—and often you're not even welcome there. It's void of sensation. It's deafening but drowned by any interaction. It cannot be staved off by music or art, no matter how collaborative. It's the knee against the breast. It's the arch of the foot on the edge of boredom tipping over the furniture. It's forgetting about children and death, dismissing both in confidence or contempt.

Alone is never having to wash your hair on an island named by your mother. You are used to the smell of yourself. Until you get sick. Time is measured by what's outside the window. And one is reminded to inhale by the cigarette and tick,tick,tick,tick,tick,tick, *breathe,* says the second hand.

Alone is never without vice: knitting, ice cream, brandy, pink plastic margarita blenders on the credit card, and empty bowls lined with popcorn grease, with slippery layers of understanding and self-pity enmeshed, entangled, one pleasing the other, the other wanting more.

It is input and recognition. *Alone* is the time one has to change the world and to think, or integrate, or study, or believe. It's not too bad for a little while. It is forever until someone's eyes meet yours.

There's a time before the choices are made when we

can all be friends.

MY CHAMBERED NAUTILUS

Haven't you begun to believe
in the twisting fate of this wet
world? Always between building
up, breaking free, and starting
again. That's love swim, you know,
you and me beginning.

Brown striped cream. Your hair,
your skin and eyes. And I
watched with such admiration as
you neatly sewed the bubble day's
film onto the walls of your
circle world. You take such care
with the sunshine of things.

People may be barnacle fools and
cut your feet with their parasite
quick kind of (open close open)
habit world, eating their surroundings.

Snatching up the world's
fastest times and making
your irregular life so hard.

But you have moved on again, haven't
you? On to the next little room.
I can't imagine in there with you
learning me. I can only see the
afterward. Broken open and dry.
But I'll bet it's all fleshy pink
joy, inside. Filling up new
between the getting-harder walls.

Boys and girls have nothing
thoughts between them all the
time. You know. Just like us.
And there is slippery understanding
there, in the Between, and the Around, and the
Just-where-you-can't-quite-reach place.
And then I begin to know a you having
nothing to do with me. A you so
resolute and confined. A you still opening
in tolerable nacre carrels, which harbor
your broad Everything.

No such skin for any of it. Spirals; or

words falling short from the way

it all could be. And then that's

good enough for a while.

I'm washing the dishes and

listening to a bit

of the evening

news on a Tuesday, I think.

PAY GRADE

I found a sealed manila envelope addressed to SPC Nathalie Jones. SPC is an army rank that means *specialist*. I've never understood it. But there it is in the chain of command between all the sorts of privates and sergeants. I opened the envelope and found three pieces of paper. The first was a letter of apology from the personnel section of my unit. Apparently I had been awarded, but there was no time to acknowledge me personally. So I was getting my award in the mail.

The second piece of paper was a bit thicker and was embossed with the bright words, "Department of the Army Certificate of Achievement." This decoration, although flattering, had very much the same appearance as the ones that are given to third graders after spelling bees or to the bad swimmers after a year of unsuccessful but dutiful competition.

The last piece of paper, dated 4 October 1998, was the most interesting. It was a thin piece of vellum with boxes, lines, numbers, and important people's signatures. This, DA form 638, Nov 94, was the proof of my award intended for addition to my permanent record. Most of it is bureaucratic nonsense so I will spare you. But the last part is interesting. And if you don't mind my bragging a bit I will recount what my superiors have written in their recommendation for my award:

Part III -- Justification and Citation Data (Use specific bullet examples of meritorious acts or service)

Achievement #1

Soldier's knowledge and experience helped maintain the high state of readiness during Operation Scout, even against incredible odds for a potentially "Unsuccessful Mission."

Achievement #2

Soldier's professionalism and sterling personal example set the pace for the entire operation as demonstrated during an unfortunate accident involving an M939, 5-ton truck rollover.

Achievement #3

The mission could easily have been scrubbed if not for soldier's tireless efforts and dedication.

Achievement #4

Soldier received on-site verbal communication by the 88th Regional Support Group BG [brigadier general] Bauerle, for the most outstanding static display out of nine displays.

Proposed Citation

For dedication during Operation Scout. Her actions demonstrated high morale and characteristic courage to drive on against incredible odds. Her devotion to duty is in the finest tradition of the military and reflects great credit upon her, this unit and the United States Army Reserves.

The commander did downgrade the recommendation from the Army Accommodation Medal to a Certificate of Achievement in spite of the whole brigadier general thing, but I feel as though I have been recognized. The military has a long tradition of glorifying those individuals who come nearest to death, and I was plenty close enough. Still, it seems odd that I have been honored for being in a vehicular accident and then going back to work, which that day meant showing up at a recruiting tent for the Boy Scout Jamboree. None of this is logical to me. Of course I went back to work. I had nowhere else to go. But regardless this award has given me much pride.

It certainly does make up for the fact that they never did figure out the paperwork to reimburse me for the medical bills. It was unnecessary but precautionary medical treatment involving being picked up by a gorgeous beefy-armed fireman, a ride through two counties in an ambulance, one four-by-four-inch piece of gauze, a small packet of Betadine, and a few good hours of eavesdropping on the guy next door who had fallen out of his wheelchair during the Indy marathon and kept screaming for his plastic surgeon.

GIVE HER WHAT SHE WANTS

Foot Foot Foot Foot Foot Foot

Footfootfootfootfootfootfeotfeetfeetfeetfeetfe

"I want an emerald," she said. And he began to run, the miner not the thief. Bare feet chasing the forest floor and his blood running after him. One fist with his livelihood, the other to protect his life. Feet of running and roving through density, green and soft-soiled.

And here he is with a knife against my throat and the blood comes dark red. It's too hot for this. The insects are here already, swarming me. I'm covered in slag from the mine and my feet are cut scars from the sharp chips of rock. He stands above me, heaving. He's too fat to run so fast. Too fat to mine himself. Not like me. I'm tiny and quick. But tired and hungry. And sick of running.

I cannot swallow the blood at my throat. I look up past him to the canopy of trees and wonder if there really is a sun.

The worn leather bag falls easily from my fatigue. And he snatches up its contents. Fourteen this time. Not as many as I've had before. But plenty more than usual.

He knew it. He knew I did well in the mines last night or he would have chased someone else.

I cannot breathe through the blood at my throat and turn over to let it drain onto the forest floor.

And he leans over to watch me die. Maybe he feels bad. But this isn't personal. This is business.

The business of adorning pretty, stupid girls with their Walgreens hair and their thick asses and the lines, with emeralds.

Emeralds are a dangerous business. I knew that.

But, even though she is so very far away in her southwest suburban household, I heard her, pouting, say to him at Christmas, "I want an emerald." And so someone had to get it for her.

breathbreathbreathbreath breath breath

breath breathbreath brea th

THE MOBILE

I woke up with the world folded in half and wondered what to do. This could not have happened at a more inopportune point in time. It was on that day that I was to receive a visit from an extraordinary friend of mine. She lives in New Zealand. I have been in love with her for quite some time now, I suppose. Embarrassing as it is, I am quite attracted to the fact that she spends the greater portion of her day with sheep.

I have not been able to fully comprehend what it is that she does. She is something of a mystery. It seems her work is half shepherd, half art. Well now, I suppose the term *art* might be going a bit overboard, but just saying that she makes things from fleece is an understatement. The last time she was here she brought me a sphere of the stuff. It was rather hefty and upon first receipt of it I could not in any way discern what it could mean.

She was rather offended, pointing out the striking—no, I believe she used the word *vivid*; yes, she said *vivid* because I remember thinking it stupid or maybe native to New Zealand to say *vivid resemblance* where I most certainly would have employed the very familiar *striking resemblance*.

Now what was it I was saying?

Oh, yes. She was rather offended when I did not immediately see the object for what it was: a model of the moon. But okay, once she had indicated this I was rather amazed to find it so accurate. Somehow she had taken the wool of sheep and created the moon complete with darker fleece for the dark side and the Sea of Tranquility. I suppose it was then I knew I was in love.

But of course she had to return to New Zealand almost immediately. Her art, in particular her beautiful herd of sheep, could not survive outside New Zealand. She returned, promising only that she would think of me often—never enough, you know—and making me promise the moon's security.

Six months after, I received a sizable package and noticed her address on the return label. For two weeks the box sat under my Christmas tree (I always put up a Christmas tree) even though it was well into January before that box ever came. Before tending to my own affairs in the morning I would sit there in that chair for a few minutes contemplating the box and its contents. It made the winter seem to melt away from this Michigan extremity.

I do not mind my job. I have my own small shop. You may have seen it across from the medical/dental pavilion with that rather slipshod awning. No, not that one. Two doors down. I suppose you might miss it what with the door somewhat recessed, but there it is. Yes, you're right. The one with *Danny's* painted on the glass. So I do not mind my job. But it is sometimes very hard to convince myself that the doors of my tiny market will ever open against the snow.

So I rather cherished those mornings, sitting with a cup of tea staring at the box. There was no doubt that a work of art was enclosed, and even more absolute perhaps was the fact that it contained wool. Hundreds of options ran through my head. I thought it might be a three-dimensional map of her town or my street or of any of the places we have visited together. And it could have been a figure from the ballet. She has an affection for ballet. She decorates her home (I have never visited but there is no reason to doubt her) with trinkets from the ballet.

She says her father had a habit of keeping her close to home. Of course there was the farm and the sheep, but as a child she saw him as a tyrant for never letting her take ballet.

In the end my curiosity conquered my imagination, and I opened the box. It seemed to be filled with beautiful ornamental balls for the tree. I was disappointed that I had not opened it immediately since two days before I had decided to take the tree down for fear of fire. Now here was this box filled with ornaments that would have to wait another year. Such an aggravation.

But as I began to pull one of the most beautiful orbs I found there was great resistance and that the rest of the balls were trying desperately to follow the lead of the first.

There were silver wires connecting each in a variety of ways one to another or another to the rest. As I worked to untangle the imposing mass, I tried not to wish for the other things I had imagined she had sent me. But there was little hope that I would find pleasure in such an array of yuletide finery. I felt rather ashamed of my ingratitude. It haunted me that I had given up, labeling the box, "Xmas from Mary J." And just storing it with the others in my cellar.

Two or three weeks later Mary called me. I could hear the sun in her voice. I thought of the summer there and her sheep grazing on verdant hills. Our conversation encompassed several things but she had obviously called in reference to the gift and I was agitated as to how I could express my feelings without offending hers.

After a pause which was most likely very expensive from her side of the world to mine, she said, "Well, Danny? What did you think of your model?"

Since I was six virtually everyone I had ever known called me Daniel. In fact I remember no terms of endearment at all. Sometimes my mother would call me Daniel Gustavo, but I believe this was only to hear together the two names she had chosen for me. She seemed to need to reassure herself that the unlikely combination of my first and middle names had not after all been a mistake.

But Mary called me Danny. She has always called me Danny. And she still does.

Without thinking or planning my next sentence I heard my reply, "My what?"

"You didn't get my gift? And here I was so angry with you for not thanking me. You didn't even get it. Mail is so awkward at Christmas. I do hope it is not entirely lost. I worked on it for almost a year. And I thought of it ages before that."

Although it would have been rather simple at that point to avoid telling her what I actually thought of the gift I could not in good conscience do so. "No, Mary. I received it some time ago. I kept it wrapped up for a period of weeks having some fun in a guessing game. But it seems even with it open I have guessed wrong. I had presumed you sent me a box of ornaments for my tree."

Her laughter sounded more like a bleating sheep than I had remembered. Maybe it was my momentary avarice. "Not tree ornaments, love. That's the sky. Didn't you read the card?"

I had not.

I carried the phone into the basement and opened the box for a second, more informed inspection. She was extraordinary. Mercury, Pluto, Jupiter, Mars. How could I have mistaken Saturn's rings for an abstractly-rendered halo?

She must have guessed I had tangled them terribly. "If you pull up gently on the sun the others will, or at least they should, just drop into place."

I did this and held up a glorious mobile. So many moons, and I had to ask how long it had taken her to string the seemingly thousands of fuzzy bits depicting the asteroid belt. I could not hide my incredulity and I believe it quite flattered her. She hesitated at first, saying that I must think it awful since I had not even recognized Earth. But after hearing my praise she shared with me several very interesting pieces of trivia which she had become aware of while researching the solar system and which facts were all apparently represented in her masterpiece.

With some instruction I had no trouble seeing any of them.

We talked every few weeks after that and wrote as often. She realized I couldn't very well lock the doors to my little shop and go to New Zealand just for a personal visit. But in due time she found a friend who was willing to take care of the farm for a few weeks in exchange for what seemed to me to be an excessive demand of mutton and fleece. I was horrified to think of three baby lambs being slaughtered for my benefit, however indirect. But Mary seemed happy with the trade and informed me she would be coming in October.

I made arrangements for her as best I could. The carpet cleaners came, and I enlisted the high school boy from across the hall to fix my shower. I bought a few clothes. At first I had chosen four new shirts, but realizing that she would immediately see my efforts to impress her I limited my purchases to one white shirt with double button sleeves and one without. I spoke with a sales representative in the necktie department but could not quite find something I liked, assuming she was opposed to yellow dots which I expected she was since I was so surprised to find that I myself had liked them.

For three weeks before she was to come all I did was sit very cautiously in my apartment trying very carefully not to get anything dirty. And I suppose just to shock me with some superstitious meaning, only days before her arrival the Earth fell from its silver strand. It landed where the dog could find it and I heard him from the other room rasping and choking with intermittent whines. He solicited my pity and I stroked him gently as he coughed against whatever it was he had found. But when I finally looked into his mouth I found it was full of wool.

I ran into the next room and found the Earth on the floor, wet and drawn. "Shit. And she's coming so soon." After the thing dried I sat with glue and rearranged a bit of the South American continent, mimicking its geography to the best of my recollection. It was certainly not the same, and there was no doubt in my mind she would notice but I hung the Earth again with several pieces of fishing line and hurried off to meet her plane.

FOR THE MAN WHO BOUGHT ME COFFEE AND WAS SHOT IN THE HEAD SOON AFTER

I have seen your

smile often tonight

lying on the freezer floor.

Did you know it would

happen when you pulled

up a chair and called me

beautiful?

Did you put a prayer

in my little white cup?

Were you talking to strangers

(funny to think me strange)

to avoid your thoughts?

You knew they were

coming, didn't you?

But you didn't know when.

So much like the rest of us
but sooner.

Was I safe to you
or did I look naive and happy?
Were you just glad someone would
go on?

And the thought of you—
who flattered me with no reserve,
wanted absolutely nothing,
and felt so good—
kneeling down with a couple of
friends in the freezer
(one on either side, I'll bet)
hands tied behind your back
looking at the door.
Hoping someone would come for you.
Wishing they hadn't.

And why did they come?
I suppose it's rude to ask.

Scared. Were you scared?
How long did you kneel there

with their words over you?
I'm glad it was cold.
I hope you were numb for your
execution.
I certainly hope you were.

I don't know why I didn't hear you
cry out. Voice submerged
by always-on-top-flattery,
beautiful faces, French,
and laughing cigarettes.

But I do remember your leaning
closer than I might have expected.
and I do remember your looking into
my eyes, hiding something
precious in me.

Anyway,
Thank you for the coffee
and for stabbing your smile
deep enough.

HOLLACE AND SOME GIRL

Black shoes need shining at the airport and grab a newspaper too. Hollace Dupree sat behind his paper not so much reading it as thanking it for dividing him from the throngs of travelers and from the shoeshiner. At page fourteen, he thought slowly whether he should have a glass of orange juice or a nice cup of coffee before his flight. Both would cost way too much, but he was above taking a thermos to the airport and actually hadn't thought of that until just now. He hated flying coach. The complimentary beverages on the plane could not be trusted unless carbonated. Airplane coffee was mealy and the orange juice often had a metallic taste or worse, had to be consumed from a miniscule plastic tub.

After nodding, smiling, and tipping the burly shoeshiner in a grand act of escape, Mr. Dupree strode across the wide corridor breaking through streams of early-morning travelers without much notice to family integrity, shopping bags bearing the visages of cartoon characters, or the momentum of gaggles of flight attendants with their wheeled carry-ons. All the various looks of disgust were lost on Hollace Dupree who moved through life from one destination to another head down and inattentive to others. Coffee. Small. Black. Thank you.

Once seated on the plane after a suitable wait at the gate and the usual boarding of the vessel by rows starting from the rear, Hollace Dupree watched the airport staff from his window without interest. He kept an eye on the conveyor belt half hoping to catch sight of his own bags being loaded onto the plane. He was uneasy and thought that if his bags were on the plane then he was certainly going to the right place.

As interesting as the search for his luggage was, it was the men who were working under the plane that eventually held his attention. The gloves and the uniforms and the grease were all such glorious accessories to the fuel lines, baggage carts, meal trucks, and so on which were teeming around the huge jet. A man holding fluorescent flashlights stood back from the crowd adjusting his knee pads. His brown curls set themselves free of a cap and then disappeared again, sweating. As the jet engines began to roar several of the workers, pulling off gloves and turning their faces toward the cold morning sun, laughed together over something easily understood while wearing ear protection.

Upon witnessing their laughter Hollace felt himself the intruder. He looked away quickly not having meant any harm. He concentrated instead on the crease in his pants, pinching it together at various points and assuring its crisp respectability. Then he turned to the safety card for a minute and focused thoughts about a water landing. It seemed an impossibility that his seat could in any way become a flotation device. Some child had left a drawing in the seat pocket. It was a bawdy array of ogres and what might have passed for either a princess or a rather sick-making pile of fruit. Hollace reviewed the sheet from several perspectives and replaced it gingerly behind the onboard catalog. He ran his finger across the bendable wire that would close the bag which Mr. Dupree had always thought suited popcorn more than human emesis. His eyes avoided the window. But he decided that once the plane was on the runway it would be okay to watch during takeoff. For now he just waited.

It was a business flight in 1999. Virtually every passenger had some combination of the following items: power suit, laptop computer, Wall Street Journal, important-looking data sheets, stapled piles of something or other to review, and coffee. Hollace Dupree was not an exception. Hollace Dupree was never an exception. He wore a gray suit and a white shirt. His tie was interesting but conservative and most likely was purchased in a department store. He had not traveled beyond what his business required, and this morning he was returning home from somewhere else. He did not have gifts to take home for anyone and would not consider finding anyone for whom to take gifts home. Hollace unknowingly defined himself through his career. He attended charity functions with clients, played golf and tennis with clients, went to an Episcopal church to meet new clients, and sent sympathy cards when his clients passed away. He was an accountant.

Without another thing to look at in order to pass the time, Hollace wondered whether it were worth soliciting some amenity from the airline woman who was near enough to be asked. But as he tried to decide between creamer which he didn't need for the coffee or a pillow which would take up too much of his tiny allotment of space, the flight attendant's attention was drawn toward the front of the plane.

Hollace looked to see what could possibly have preempted his needs.

Never had he witnessed such an abomination. There, on the rubber mat outside the cockpit, stood a girl. Not so unremarkable even on a 6:07 a.m. business flight, but this girl was wearing a hot pink gown with hoop skirts.

The skirt must have been made with at least fifteen yards of material and there was bulk and fluff added by several layers of crinolines and other undergarments. The skirt was accompanied by an extremely tight bodice. There were times when women had ribs removed to fit themselves into such bodices, and one wondered whether this girl had required such an operation. Several vertical shafts seemed to run through the bodice. And a panel of white muslin was brought together in an even more restraining manner by a network of ribbons. The supposed concept of this invention was that it allowed her bosom to sit so precariously that it might at any time happen to fall into plain view.

She boarded the plane at 6:05 a.m. in a fit of rage. Her arms were flying around her, at one moment wiping away tears, at another tugging at the skirt that would not fit into the aisle. And those same arms seemed to reflect utter despair which required much attention. She snapped at the flight attendant. "What—? Do you have a problem? You could help me, you know, you and your polyester-perfect polka dot bow tie. What is up with that bow tie? How do you get that ridiculous ribbon so tangled around your neck and make it look intentional? Huh? And that manicure too. Red. You have all those same red nails. Do you think I want to stare at your red nails and your gold rings and your hair-sprayed French twists when I'm flying to Toronto? Do you?"

This was long enough before 9/11 that members of the flight crew had not fully relinquished their servile roles in favor of a more enforceable intimidation. And too bad, really; much might have been different. But as it was, the flight attendant ran her tongue over her teeth and swallowed twice before she replied in a pleasant but firmly kind voice, "I'm afraid we are not destined for Toronto this morning, ma'am. Do you require assistance finding another gate? We would like to push back as soon as possible."

The girl dropped her arms to her sides and stared into the flight attendant with black eyes. "There are a thousand small trolls like you rushing into life this morning in high heels. And do you know what? Color contacts are made with the rotting placentas of rabbits."

The flight attendant receded somehow, coughing back tears with her hand unconsciously patting her upswept hair.

The woman in the pink dress succumbed to the rage and began a public fit of sobbing tears.

"My lord." Hollace whispered to himself with incredulity, awe, and embarrassment.

The girl was a disgrace. Her hair was disheveled but looked a recent bouncing mane of banana curls. She wore gloves and lace and ribbons and bows. Gaudy pewter and glass jewelry seemed an awful burden but sporadically flashed rainbows around the cabin as she thrashed against the lavatory door. On top of all this she was wearing a dark green backpack covered with embroidery, strange patches, and small activist pins. But the ensign of her absolute displacement from the nineteenth century was that she had a tattoo of small roses that wrapped around her biceps. She kept sobbing with such overt pain that women found themselves disgusted by the trails of her mascara, and men watched her heaving chest with high hopes.

Several minutes passed. No one wanted to take control of the situation. The flight attendants certainly would not and the pilots did their best to busy themselves with knobs and gauges. The other passengers furtively looked past their papers hoping to catch a quip or anecdote from the girl. Each was planning a witty icebreaker to explain his or her late arrival. An apple-cheeked maniac escaping the throes of antebellum society and flinging obscenities is certainly a better story than the usual broken fuel lines and fog delays.

Finally realizing that the aisle could not possibly be negotiated in all her finery, the girl began to tug wildly at the skirts. And she left behind her a pile of crinoline, hot pink taffeta, and at least three bone hoops which the flight attendant nearest to her heaped into a storage bin generally reserved for strollers.

The girl stood in bloomers looking for a seat. She scratched her leg with the opposite foot. She was wearing black stockings and black boots with laces that crisscrossed themselves halfway up to her knee. There were uncomfortable laughs, shakes of voyeurs' papers, and the tsks and gasps which are generally heard at such times.

Hollace, choosing the lesser of two evils, allowed his eyes to go back to the men outside. He took his chances that they might notice his vicariously enjoying their fun.

The girl, still crying uncontrollably, flung herself toward the empty seat in the 14th row. As if to assure the other passengers that she had a right to be there, she sat down next to Hollace Dupree with a deliberate flounce, settled herself, and after kicking him more than once she was established there and cried freely. She leaned against the seat in front of her sobbing breathlessly.

Hollace sat braced in his seat. Every muscle in his body was tense with her proximity. Though he was concerned for her happiness he was also concerned with his own, and he could smell her. From the corner of his eye he could see the line of pale flesh that ran from her elbow along the curve of her armpit and up over her breast as she sat with her arms folded on top of the seat in front of her. He could also sense her thighs through the thin wrinkles of the muslin bloomers.

Just as she could not stop crying to breathe, Hollace Dupree could not possibly lift the weight of restraint from his own breast in order to catch some air.

He swallowed hard several times and felt his Adam's apple against the tight collar. He pursed his lips and relaxed them again. He tilted his head, up and back, up and back, all the while looking out the window. The back of his neck was hot, surely a result of air not circulating well through the synthetic materials from which airplane headrests tend to be made. His eyebrows danced between wide-eyed inspection and fervent disapproval. And although so much motion was occurring above his shoulders, from the neck down he was clenched. His left hand held his pants so tightly that the carefully-placed crease was dying by strangulation under his grip.

Around them the passengers still regarded the girl with some fear. Not because she looked abnormal, but because the entire plane echoed with her dramatic crying. By this time she was beating the seat in front of her with a small fist and screaming, "No. You fucking jackass bastard! No. God damn it. No!" Over and over and over again. And wailing through her tears in such a way that the flight attendants retreated to the ends of the cabin in two closely-huddled groups and unconsciously spun their heavy wedding bands around bony red-nailed fingers. One of the women went into the restroom, took off her bow tie, and retied it altogether. Those passengers who were sitting nearby became such a shifting mass of energy that static electricity built as frictive pantyhose and wool pants rubbed against fireproof synthetic seats.

The copilot quickly slammed the door that divided the flight crew from the cabin. Even though there were no reassuring or informative announcements, the plane started and the pilots began to recover the few lost minutes. The plane shifted with anticipation and began to roll out of the gate, but there was no sign that the girl would ever stop crying. It was apparent all other parties were diligently avoiding the situation, which left Hollace Dupree alone to comfort the poor thing, although it was hard to feel sorry for someone so violent.

Drawing in a quick breath to sustain his determination he prioritized his possible courses of action. At the office he might offer her a cup of coffee, water, or even juice. He could allow her to sit at his desk for a few minutes to quiet herself. However, they were not at the office. He considered the situation. There seemed so few resources. He might offer her the window seat, but that seemed excessive. He decided instead upon, "Hello there. Hmm. Let's see. Here's my card."

Now, this might not have been the most tactful thing to say, but Hollace Dupree was practiced at the statement and knew he could rely on it for a response. He wasn't sure his sentimental skills would project confidence. The girl, it seemed at first, reacted positively. In one motion she cast the backpack onto the floor in the aisle, ran her sweaty hands over her face several times, threw herself against her own seat back, and grabbed the card.

Rendon and Associates Inc.
Hollace Dupree, CPA
Outstanding Balance and Property
Humbly serving the community since 1964

Having read the card and with the stultifying shock of its presentation wearing off, the girl replied, "Don't you want to know why I'm in such a fucking fit? Why do you people always think about business? I mean for God's sake I need some humanity here. Look at me. Do you think I'm going to need a—." She looked at the card for some evidence of his position. "Whatever you are? I'm a complete wreck, and all you can think of is how you can score one for your business? I hate you."

Hollace decided that while he probably should have offered her the window seat initially, he certainly would not do so now. This girl was a defiant creature. "Always thinking about scoring and business." The thought! What he would do for any other seat on that plane. His character did not allow him to make such a request now. But this was too much.

The girl continued her attack. "What are you anyway? Going off to some rich business brunch. Going to look at some expensive graphs and eat catered food off of paper plates. Or are you going to go back to your wife after a night of fucking your whore in another city? Don't forget to put your wedding ring back on, asshole."

"I am not married." Hollace drew his handkerchief out of his pocket and patted his face. Though the cabin was cool he seemed to be sweating.

"Oh, I get it. So you like it from the boys down in the mailroom. I should have known. Fucking handmade pointy shoes. You're wearing purple socks, for Christ's sake."

The socks along with the tie which Hollace was wearing had been a present from his sister-in-law the previous Christmas. In any event he knew that neither was purple; they were, in fact, plum. His sister-in-law had assured him they were not purple. Hollace Dupree would never wear purple socks. These were definitely plum.

The plane was just completing its ascent. Hollace had completely missed takeoff. He was incensed.

Sitting up straighter and turning toward the girl he asked, "Is there anything that I might do to protect myself against this early-morning tirade?"

The girl was taken aback. She looked around for her defense. No one supported her. The other passengers were busy with their papers and coffee, listening. "You know why I'm on this plane? Because this is the gate where my friend was working. She works at the counter for this airline, and she gave me a boarding pass. We go out all the time and she always says that if I want to go somewhere I should just come to the counter where she works and she'll slip me on the plane. So here I am. I don't know where this plane is even going. And you know what? I don't have to, because I don't care."

Hollace decided from this obvious display of insecurity that the girl was probably around twenty-three years of age— old enough to have serious problems but still too young to handle them by herself. He was regaining strength.

She adjusted her bodice.

Hollace watched her writhing long enough to decide that she must be exceedingly uncomfortable. Then, without daring to try, he wished he had looked a little longer.

As though she had come full circle by that statement, she returned to his question. "Yes. You can. If you want me to shut up you can tell me why all men are such assholes."

Maybe only twenty-one judging from the overwhelming generalization. "Do you mean any particular man, because I certainly cannot speak for us all?" Hollace tried not to smile at the girl. He wanted her to be assured that he was taking her plight seriously.

She saw the kindness in his eyes. "Okay, well then, Jake. Tell me why Jake is such an asshole."

"Jake of Jake's Lawn Care or Jake of Jake's Pizza?"

A beautiful young pink smile. "Jake of my asshole ex-boyfriend cheating ass, Jake."

"Oh. Not an entrepreneur of the usual sort, I see."

"More usual than you think, Mr. —," again consulting the business card, "Dupree."

"I suppose this is so."

"You never cheated on a girlfriend?"

Hollace considered the question. After dismissing a confusing incident in college that may have fit the definition of infidelity but certainly was a misunderstanding by all parties, he decided to go with his statistical average which was a decided, "No."

"Why not?"

Oh. These questions. Why not look out over the billow of cloud that spread out to the horizon making the view from the window a treasure for a moment? It was only six in the morning. Why not look at the sunrise? What a rare thing to be so close to it. Why think about some foolish young man 30,000 feet below and miles behind? He avoided the question since she was obviously torturing herself. Self-inflicted romance problems are prominent at nineteen—but she must be older than that.

"I never cheated on a girlfriend because I never considered the stuff of romance to be a game. One might cheat at cards and board games, not in relationships. Relationships are business. Negotiation and respect. Always took it as serious business, I'm afraid. May I ask a question of you, Miss—?" He solicited her last name.

"Well, as of one thirty this morning it's Mrs. Jake Russell. We eloped."

Definitely twenty-two. "Well, Mrs. Russell—"

"Don't call me that. He's such a rat bastard."

"Regardless of your name then, why did you board the plane this morning in such antiquated attire?"

She tore at the dress's narrow cap shoulders. She pulled off some cheap earrings and wiped her nose in a disgusting manner with the back of her hand. "I fucking hate my job. Do you know that I have four of these dresses? And on the Fourth of July I have to wear one that is all red, white, and blue, with stars and a fucking patriotic parasol. Eight years. First I sold lemonade. That wasn't so bad. I smoked cigarettes with all the Mexicans and only had to wear some stupid paper pioneer hat. I work at Merton Village and Historic Theme Park. It's awful.

"Now I'm the folly girl in the cafe where they serve cotton candy and popcorn to a bunch of little kids. Jake is a blacksmith. He makes all sorts of stupid trinkets out of old nails and sells them all for about seventy-five times what they're worth. So after work yesterday we went out like we always do—two and a half years. He told me to meet him by the blacksmith shop and we rode his motorcycle over to the water and got married by a gambling boat captain. Nice wedding. Can you believe I stayed with that dick for two and a half years?"

Her vulgar language was beginning to wear on Hollace. He winced.

"Sorry. Are you like my mom's age or what?"

Hoping he was much younger than the mother and closer in fact to the age of the girl, Hollace hedged, "Well, how old is your mother?"

"I don't know. I never met her. It's just a figure of speech, you know."

Hollace didn't know. He had no idea in fact. "Yes. I suppose so."

The flight attendant appeared with the beverage cart. Hollace asked politely about the brand of orange juice and requested a ginger ale as well, if it weren't too much trouble. The girl ordered a Bloody Mary with four extra shots of vodka. Hollace noticed that the stewardess ignored the alcohol limit. Everyone on the plane was indebted to Hollace for dealing with the girl. There was a look of thanksgiving. Noting this and in a fit of generosity Hollace whipped out his wallet and paid for the girl's drinks.

"You didn't need to do that." She pulled at the plastic on the lid of the vodka with her teeth. Once she had ripped the cellophane and spit it onto the floor she dumped half the vodka into her drink and drank the rest straight.

He watched her with a combination of sickness and intrigue. "It is your wedding day. It's the least I can do." It is true that Hollace was interested in hearing the rest of this story. "So who is the harlot?"

"The what?"

"Jake's other—well, the other woman."

"Oh, the cheap-ass whore?"

"Having never met her, I'll reserve my judgment. But for the purposes of discussion and clarity, yes, the—well, the cheap-ass whore." Hollace was proud of himself. And smiled with closed lips.

They both laughed and toasted each other. Hollace was careful not to spill his half-filled glass, and her drink sloshing wildly ran over onto the back of her hand. She sucked the liquid quickly and licked her entire hand clean. Hollace thought this was obscene and found himself intently tapping his index finger on the tray. He finished his drink and slowly poured another small amount of juice into his class.

After opening a packet of peanuts and swallowing the entire contents without really chewing, the girl went on. "Well. God knows what her name is. People call her Bitsy. Isn't that disgusting? She's no one. She takes tickets at the Scrambler. Big hair. Bad jeans. You've seen a thousand like her at places like that. Real skinny, you know?"

Hollace adjusted the vent above his head so that more air was flowing over him. "I guess I'm not a big fan of amusement parks. Wouldn't know the type most likely, I'm afraid."

The girl nodded. "Right. She's trash, if you want to know the truth." Without asking permission the girl poured one of the tiny vodka bottles into Hollace's cup. "Have a screwdriver, Hollace Dupree. You need it after listening to all this crap. Besides you paid for it."

He did not refuse. He probably couldn't have.

There was a lull in their conversation through a bit of turbulence. They kept drinking for a few quiet minutes. Hollace looked out over the white cloud bank that undulated under them and reflected sunlight everywhere. He thought of Jake somewhere down there. Just married and wondering where his wife was on an overcast day. What a glorious morning. What an odd beginning. The girl rummaged through her backpack for something.

Thrusting some worn paper and a strip of photos from a picture booth the girl, like a television lawyer, burst out, "See. Look at this shit. After we got married he wanted to take me to a hotel but I was cold so he let me wear his jacket on the bike. These were in the pocket. I jumped off the bike when he was going almost twenty miles an hour. I grabbed a bottle of Jack from a shitty little convenience mart and just got a cab right to the airport."

Hollace looked at the pictures. They verged on pornographic. He wondered why this girl married such a rather ugly young man. She was very pretty and judging from these photographs he was not an all up to her standard. His mind wandered as he stared blankly at the pictures. How could she possibly ride a motorcycle in that bizarre dress? Resolutely he informed her, "You could do much better than this boy. I suggest getting an annulment."

"A what?"

"An annulment. Void your marriage. Have it taken away. Erased."

"But I love him."

Hollace said nothing. He held the strip of pictures up for her to see.

Tears formed in her eyes and she took the liberty of ripping Hollace's breast pocket handkerchief from his suit and blowing her nose in it. "It's so cheap to just quit. I want to work it out. What if that didn't mean anything to him? He loves me, you know."

Not quite believing her, Hollace refrained from pointing out that running from the situation might not be how to work it out. "Some things are not worth fighting for. Sometimes, on days like this, one must simply assess the situation and resolve to walk away. Simply let the oppressive nature of the situation be what it is and submit to it." Hollace finished his drink resolutely. "Then, and it will no doubt be in short order, you will rise above the thing to new heights. And you will be the better for it."

"You're one of those people that think every bad experience just builds character and crap like that, huh?" "

"Possibly." He did not like feeling cornered.

"I'm more of the 'shit happens' school myself."

Nodding repeatedly in a mildly drunken state, Hollace showed his understanding.

"Or maybe I should just go balls out and fuck somebody raw. Don't you think? Then we'd be even. Then we could just go on." She recanted when she saw he was shocked. "Annulment. Yeah. I guess. How do you get it?"

Hollace explained what little he knew and gave the names of service offices that should certainly be able to give her assistance. He was a resourceful man.

They bought two more drinks and talked about her options as the flight made headway through what breath we share.

"But it's so embarrassing. God. It's so embarrassing."

Hollace pointed out that throwing tantrums in hoop skirts on an airplane might be in a similar vein. The girl, obviously drunk, laughed. They laughed together about their first impressions of each other. Hollace explained how thoroughly she had drawn the attention of every other passenger. The girl was uplifted by the story and pleased that people had been paying attention to her. She swore she had been unaware. Maybe twenty-four. The girl apologized for making fun of his purple socks. They most certainly were plum. And besides, she liked them.

The girl decided to change into something more normal so her sister wouldn't freak out when she met her at the gate. The plane began its descent.

He complimented her tattoo. They talked easily as she unlaced her boots. He commented on the dexterity she had with the laces and she reminded him how long she had been wearing them. She showed him the blisters the boots caused and he noticed the silver ring on her second toe. It had been a gift from a friend. It was from Athens. The friend went to Greece every year with her grandmother to visit her great aunt. Hollace listened and stared at the toes that she wiggled over his lap. Ten toes with rosy gold polish.

She stood up in the aisle organizing her bag and digging to the bottom for a pair of jeans. She leaned over the bag. Hollace watched her. Her springy curled hair danced around her shoulders. Sitting against the seat had caused them to become ridden with static electricity and more tangled. Hollace imagined this might be what she should have looked like anyway, waking up after her wedding night. He looked at the way her neck stopped and spilled out over the collar bone and ran into two simple reservoirs, her breasts, caught in the cups of that strange 19th century bodice. Without thinking he reached out and ran his finger from her chin down over them. She jerked her head up. They stared at one another.

"So beautiful." His lower lip was caught by his teeth.

The girl grabbed her clothes and went to the bathroom to change.

Hollace was unsure what had just happened. He did not meet the gaze of the older woman across the aisle and instead turned his face to the window, to the back of the seat in front of him, to the tray-table's latch, then into the seat next to him where the girl's backpack sat agape. A bra hung out from the bag. Hollace put the bra into the bag, touching it with deference, and looked out the window. He felt the pressure change in his ears. They were going down quickly.

When she returned the girl sat straight in the chair, seat belt fastened, legs crossed away from him, flipping through the onboard catalog without seeing the merchandise. Hollace wished there was something he could say. His fingers ran up and down along the crease of his pants. He pursed his lips repeatedly and tried to breathe against the constraints of his collar around his Adam's apple. The plane landed with a mild jolt.

Nothing was said.

Still seated, the girl was ready with her backpack on as they taxied to the gate. Hollace waited to retrieve his briefcase from under the seat. He did not wish to disturb her again. After waiting for the door to open the girl pushed her way to the front of the plane to retrieve her skirts. Hollace sighed and picked up his dirty rumpled handkerchief from her seat where it had been left, used and forgotten. He hoped she would not notice as he passed behind her at the front of the cabin.

But she saw him coming. A flight attendant was trying to make sense of the hoops and billows of material. Thankful still, the girl smiled at Hollace as she gathered her skirts from the flight attendant's arms. "Well, be off to your exploits then. And hand out a thousand of your Outstanding Balance business cards."

Allowing the bustling business people to rush past them Hollace looked at his clean black shoes. Then he cleared his throat and directed his attention toward her. "Actually no. I am afraid you will be the last to receive one. I was fired over the phone at five-thirty this morning." He put his culprit hand in his pocket and cleared his throat. "I found an error somewhere in excess of a quarter million dollars on the company books recently. Apparently the higher-ups did not appreciate my accuracy. Or perhaps having fully realized the error, they needed to downsize in order to cut costs." And he was past her, moving up the corridor with dignity. "Good luck to you, though."

The girl stood tangled in pink taffeta wishing and unwishing. She dumped the taffeta in the gate entrance and called after him, "Hollace!" He was already quite far ahead and she had to call many times. But he returned earnestly and granted her request to wait in the bar while she made a phone call. In fact made two.

"Hey, Larise. Yeah, I told Mom last night. … Of course she freaked. She gave me the whole why-can't-you-be-like-your-big-sister talk and then started crying and all that routine. … Yeah, I'm happy. Happy enough. I just didn't want to bother with putting together all the invitations and shit. … I know. … The boat thing wasn't what I had in mind either. … Well you can come out in June. We're going to have a reception and everything then when his uncle's family visits."

She looked toward Hollace. Travelers streamed through the corridor reading gate information, hugging, hurrying, showing their children the planes and the big windows, and talking. There were everyone: Indians and Blacks and Asians and Hispanics and Whites and Old People on Carts and Hollace waited for her in the bar as though he might never leave. There was nothing on the table and he seemed to be unaware of all those drinking around him. Instead his head was cocked slightly and he stared contentedly at an elevated television.

The phone conversation went on, "No, don't worry about it. That was a stupid idea. I'm at the hotel. He's asleep. I just wanted to call and tell you that I'm not really crazy enough to leave him. I just got pissed off when I found those pictures. But he said it didn't mean anything. Kind of a last fling before we got married I guess…. Yeah, I'll call you in a few days." And then she called Jake.

"I know. I know. I'm sorry. Don't cry. I'm coming home tonight and everything's going to be great. Okay? I love you, too."

She smiled as she hung up the phone. Hollace watched her pulling her wedding ring off and shoving it into the pocket of her jeans and wondered for a moment what he was getting into, but he didn't really care. He picked up her backpack and carried it on his shoulder. It looked odd next to his conservative suit. With his briefcase in the other hand, he walked upright and gray. She danced around him with curving hips and bright raggedy clothes. He paid for the taxi. She nudged him in the ribs. She rearranged his hair. She said careful things that allowed him to laugh, and easy vengeance was her consummation.

MEANING-MAKING

I am beginning to find my way along the border of life. Ducking between moments and shifting from one person's shadow to the next: sketching. I am scared and am lonely— wondering if it's a good idea. Sometimes people notice me watching. I suppose I should care—should stop maybe. But I don't. I am trying to see how far I can pursue the rest of regular life without losing these stories with their breath and heartbeats.

Writing is a careful wonder that is rarely modulated in the way one would please. Inspiration can come when production is impossible, and it can leave altogether—if indefinitely. A writer must be conscious, listening, patient, and always an invested gatherer of life. At the same time this writer must rip life from reality and position it within his or her work of art. A writer can communicate with an unknown number of strangers but, perhaps more easily, can fail utterly the moment awareness of the reader is lost.

A writer must know his or her own limitations and be willing to believe they do not exist. So the writer lives in a dream. Caught in creation's space between sleep and work, the writer seems lazy. Staying in bed for days. Leaning on comfortable bars. Drinking coffee over immovably crossed legs. But during all this time the writer is ready to give up tangible life to pursue an improbable vision with total focus and control. When the time comes to put words down, this writer must be strong enough to survive the wrangle of self with perfection, art, and isolation.

It is a bleak attitude, but a writer must be able to invest every resource in a story which may never be read. Worse than this a writer must be willing to begin with aggressive conviction knowing that the work may not come out right and very well end up abandoned, to say nothing of what else could have been done with the many hours of frustration, diligence, and ideas lost.

I am wishing all of it were better and not so bulky. I am wishing I didn't have to start so small. I resent the work no one will appreciate. And I am frightened of what I might say. Yet my dreams of writing are stale. Action on any level is preferable to regret.

And so it may be transient. It may fail. It may rip me apart. But this is the beginning of what I will write.

ON A SWELTERING SUMMER EVENING

On a sweltering summer evening when the campus at Purdue was swarming with conference attendees, Kathy Bates stopped me for directions to the armory. She was a pug-nosed woman with a peeling red face accompanied by a rotund gentleman wearing BluBlockers. I knew she was Kathy Bates because a yellow name tag hung awkwardly from her shirt.

It sucks to be lost. I said, "It's just the other side of this one. That long brick building."

To which she quickly replied, "Like all these other brick buildings?" It was acid but jovial, some mask for being snide.

Shocked and nodding, I moved on. In a voice too high-pitched to go unnoticed, the man in BluBlockers gave an apologetic thank-you over his shoulder. I walked home reminded that Purdue is one solid edifice of baked clay and wondered why a layer of gasoline swirled dirty pink translucent disruption on top of the hose-water running out from the petunia planters in front of Krannert.

DATELINE '99

The Midwest has been incredibly hot this July; I suppose partly in anticipation of the millennium. In all of this heat many people have resorted to the utilization of air conditioners. I have never been a big fan of climate control. This is not born of environmental awareness or of a fiscal nature to save tax dollars on electrical resources that are sapped by all the public offices. The fact of the matter is, and I'm rather embarrassed to say, I just think air conditioning is creepy.

So in the sweltering heat of the past month I have not had air conditioning at home or in my workplace. No air conditioning has allowed me to wallow in such a delirious state of naked inactivity that I have never found myself happier.

And whether or not it's related, I will make an effort to lose what social graces I have acquired over twenty-some years of wearing a breathtaking corset around my lips. I feel that it is best to invite the world into my true self—a crazed bitch with weird paranoia. In the words of A.D., "I'm all about salvation

… just not an army of it." So I've been saying the wrong thing in social situations more and more often. Take last night, for instance.

(Sorry for the interruption but I have just found a patch of blue fur behind my cat's ear. It seems as though she has gotten into some sort of writing utensil, possibly a broken highlighter or one of those nice liquid ink pens.)

Just last night, in an air conditioned car, I screamed, "God damn it. I'm going to spend God knows how long in a fucking coffin. Do I have to start that shit now?" At which point I began ripping at several little black plastic levers nearby, forcing the windows to perform some sort of up and down vacation bible school dance. *"Praise ye the Lord. Hallelujah. Praise ye the Lord. Hallelujah. Praise ye the Lo—"* Hmmm. However, I am glad that I said what I said. I think this is a positive advancement on my part.

Such tirades as the one I uttered in the car are generally reserved for display to my family and closest friends, but this last was directed at a woman I have just met. I suppose most accurately it was directed at the woman's car. It was one of those very clean cars that is too old to warrant being so clean. So I feel it was justified. I hate those cars.

Obviously the driver of the car was rather taken aback and took the liberty of smacking me across the face with such force that I was knocked unconscious and am unaware whether I spent the remainder of the trip locked in a sealed chamber of conditioning.

GRAND PRIX PARALLELS

Boys of the rich, sit.

Powdery gold eyes

shadowed by a man at the door,

by hats, and scaring us all

left vintage prey, and

shadowed by a cheap night riot.

Boys of the rich, sit.

Boys of the poor, look,

far away fun. The flesh seared to

a cookout afternoon. And then

open. Their hearts perforated

skeleton shells, eaten through working

virtue, easy-for-me, eyes.

Boys of the rich, sit while

boys of the poor, look, fuckable poor,

clutching sweaty drunk fists, and

by parasite faith I am the pretty

listener today for one man

playing fool-fueled

balcony games on a

cookout grill, chatting weather

stories, for me.

Not achievement, or politics, or

blood-borne fights. Just girls,

girls, girls, ugly fuckable girls, and beer.

And his disposable expense of

how (craning and wide)

I was the pretty attendant for the

sweet regular boy, who cooked

quiet and calm, with the drunken wet

(beer, beer, ugly fuckable beer)

glass shattered in patient hands.

Holding (no money wads in pockets, just)

the shards and blood alike

And proud he excused himself

(ugly, sweet)

to clean up the mess

kissing me gently on the way.

Seventeen days and the wondering time is only beginning. I should have realized long ago that forever is only a day-after-day hell that happens to the best of us. I don't know. I got the high school thing out of the way, and now it's just waiting to see where the wrinkles will go and how the flesh will fill out. The waiting time is here and I'm seventeen days in.

EMPIRE QUARRY

I remember once, at night, swimming naked in a quarry. The blackness wrapped around me with its several textures. Deep shifting moonlight supported me with waves and stroked my hair as I lay back in the lap of the water. Stone severed and scarred and hard with confining presence somewhere on all sides of me was harder than my strongest days. And the mystery of the night sky reached so very close to infinity, over and over again, with just as many stars one behind the other.

I thought about the skyline in New York. How it must be looking very much the same. How its height was nothing more than stars and its hardness no harder than here, wherever the water could go. At no wonder of that at all. Because the rock that had been where I was swimming was taken there and made into a towering piece of windows. Everyone was impressed, so many years ago.

But what of this earth? What of this hole they left? And how often do they really say it's all from Indiana? All those important people complaining about natural resources and hoarding other cultures' treasures at the same time. There I was swimming where there used to be thick impenetrable land. And that's what they did. Someone important with a dream and some money said, "Let's make the tallest building in the world."

But you cannot make tall buildings without stealing blocks from the other little boys' piles. And so they came and took our ground and left a hole. Which is good enough for cliff-dive swimming if you know where it is. It is very hard to find. Even more so at night.

LAMELLAR

"Wait. Don't freak out." Jason kneeled on the curb bent over a sewer grate. He balanced himself on his knees and hands without allowing his feet with new shoes or his new shirt to touch the street. From his maladapted Downward Facing Dog, he said, "They didn't fall that far. There's some kind of shelf or something. Maybe six feet. Or less." He leaned back and briskly slapped his hands against each other. "Jen, why don't you go in and get a hanger or something. Maybe an old shoe lace too. I don't know. Whatever looks good."

A regular-looking girl with a broken ankle nodded and went toward a white apartment house to search for the tools.

Jason turned to the other girl. She was lithe but not about to kneel in the street even if they were her keys. Instead, after she had dropped them she had stood over the grate waiting as though the key patrol would quickly be notified. She was not disappointed. This boy, Jason, and his girlfriend, Jen, had just come out of the house to see why she had been standing outside their window for so long with seemingly no agenda.

She had explained simply. "My keys have fallen." She then pointed in the general direction of her feet and it seemed to Jen that even if her keys had just fallen on the pavement and not into a sewer that she still would have waited for a considerate young man such as Jason to stop and retrieve them for her.

Jen returned with an armload of interesting objects. She laid them all on the pavement and sat on the curb with her broken foot out in the street. "I got a hanger and all this other stuff. Maybe I should go out on the balcony and get those cookout tongs."

"No." Jason thought of his grill and his hot dogs and hamburgers and chicken breasts and knew that he did not want those tongs anywhere near the sewer. "Your foot is still pretty bad. Don't bother climbing all those steps. This will be fine." He looked at her haul.

There were three old metal hangers, a pair of needle-nosed pliers, several twist-ties, a refrigerator magnet that was sizable and had a laminated postage stamp picture of Mount Rushmore on the front, a large plastic candy cane that was partially bent, a gaudy cross on a thick leather necklace most likely assembled in Sunday school by a young admirer, and a roll of electrical tape.

Jason leaned over the pile adjusting his baseball cap and trying to make sure Jen didn't catch him looking at the other girl's legs. But neither of the girls was paying any attention to him.

They were busy and casual, but dressing each other down.

"What did you say your name was?"

"Elisia."

"That's pretty."

Elisia looked over Jen from behind her black sunglasses. She looked down the street at a shop window and wondered whether she could get a bottle of water in there. She let her eyes ride back to Jen by means of a sleek Jaguar cruising up the street.

"How'd you break your leg?"

"It's not my leg."

"If it's not broken, what did you do? Sprain it?" Elisia looked at Jason and thought he was pretty good-looking. Not that good-looking but better than this Jen person deserved. She smiled as best she could with her cheeks drawn in between her teeth.

"No. It is broken. But it's my foot." Jen looked at the girl's tight skirt. The little green sausage casing was so sadly vulgar Jen almost laughed out loud. Pathetic. Blatant. Jen would give anything to have a look into Elisia's purse. What would she find? A silver cigarette case from some foreign country where she had never traveled, an expensive pen and paper too pretty to write on, and ticket stubs from all the plays that advertise in the newspaper, no doubt. Jen didn't take the bait and allow her ire to rise while Elisia stared at Jason. She just responded to the question. "Broke it Thursday at my uncle's farm."

Both the girls watched Jason assemble the contraption meant to retrieve Elisia's set of keys. He periodically looked into the sewer to reassess their location. But when he bent over the grate, his body blocked the sunlight so it was very hard for him to catch a glimpse of the keys. He crawled back and forth around the grate on his hands and knees, still keeping his feet off the ground so as not to scratch up his new shoes.

Elisia replied with pleasant disdain. "Oh. Your uncle has a farm. That must be nice."

"Yeah. He lets me board my horse there during the year when I'm here at school. It helps me get out of my head to ride."

Elisia was mildly interested by the implication of money behind the ownership of a horse. Her attention shifted from Jason to Jen. "So what happened to your foot?"

"It's stupid, really. I was up on this box brushing my horse after we got in. I just tried to reach too far behind me and twisted the whole thing over on myself. It was totally disgusting. When I turned the box to see my foot it was totally flat and bent all the way back, kind of like a hoof. Then I passed out."

Jason spoke with pieces of blue electrical tape on many of his fingers. He held the hanger contraption between his legs and balanced himself against Jen's shoulder. "Yeah, and it was just like Lassie or something. Molly, her horse, went right up to the house. Jen's aunt freaked out because she was half asleep in a chair on the porch when she felt horse breath all over her. But she went down to the barn and there was my beautiful Jen all passed out in a pile of vomit."

"Thank you, Jason, for filling in all the gruesome details." Asshole.

Elisia oversaw and Jen scooched down the curb closer to the grate as Jason began to lower his retraction device into the sewer.

Elisia stepped back from the stench. "God, that's awful."

Jen looked up at her and wondered whether her earrings were fake. "I know. Any time we open the window to get a breeze that's all we smell. One time Jason was making cookies to prove that he did know how to cook and burned all of them because he was watching wrestling and forgot them. The whole apartment filled up with this nasty smoke and a smoke alarm went off and so we opened the window. All night long that's all we smelled: sewage and burnt cookies. I still haven't had any cookies."

"Thank you for revealing all my darkest secrets to this new friend of ours." He stared at his girlfriend as if to say, "Are you that insecure, Jen? Do you really have to be such a bitch whenever there is another girl here?"

Jason leaned back to avoid the smell and to keep a patch of sunlight on Elisia's keys. He poked the hanger further into the sewer.

A voice echoed below them. "What the fuck is this?"

Jason jumped back, pulling up his device. Jen leaned over the grate and squinted into her shadow. Elisia moved toward their small porch and sat on its low brick wall in relative safety.

"Who goddamned keys is this?"

Jen whispered to Jason, "There's some guy down there."

Jason was scared and defensive. "Yeah, no shit. I was supposed to go to soccer practice today."

"What?" Jen contorted her face in hostile disgust. "Where is that coming from?"

"Jen, not now."

"Why are you always being so weird? You don't have to be at soccer practice for an hour and a half, and I don't see why you get so obsessed with all the intramural shit anyway."

"Don't I drive you to the barn to see Molly four times a week? Why is it I'm the one who's obsessed?"

The voice came from below. "Are you all bickering up there? Why you doing it over my bed? And whose keys is these?"

Jason looked at Jen. Jen shrugged and pointed to the hanger, then pointed toward the sewer.

Jason lowered the device and said cautiously as if he were a marshal with the ATF, "Sir, all you have to do is put the keys on the hook."

"Jesus. Get that shit out of my hair." Then, "And not there either. 'Bout to poke my blessed eye out with that fool thing. You want these keys, eh?"

Jen looked at Jason. "Why are we always helping people? You're talking to a guy through a sewer grate and she's not even doing anything. She's sitting on my fucking porch. I'm the one with the broken foot. And she's pulling on my plants. Get her out of here."

"You tell her to quit messing with the plants. I'm not your keeper."

Jen kept her whisper harsh. "You think she's hot is what it is. Don't even try to be all valiant whatever with me." Turning, Jen smiled and held her hand up blocking the sun. "Elisia. There's a man down here with your keys. Would you like them back?"

The girl in the tight green skirt remained on the porch and made no advance after Jen's directive. Elisia's eyes widened to a painful degree, and she seemed to be thrusting her neck wildly toward Jen as though Jen were supposed to pick up some hidden meaning. Jen pretended not to understand and completely ignored Elisia's intended efforts to dissociate herself.

But the gestures were exceedingly clear. Elisia's bobbing head said plainly, "Are you crazy? Don't tell some sewer man those are my keys. Jesus! My roommate is home. She has keys. I can copy my fucking keys. Just don't let that sewer man touch me. Dear Jesus God!" And as she realized that Jen was not picking up her vibes there were the added insinuations of, "You are the most conniving bible banging bitch I've ever seen. I'd give anything if you saw your precious boyfriend blasting some angel from the choir. Are you really this stupid? Forget the fucking keys."

And with this Elisia hid her purse carefully behind Jen's planters. She took off her watch, her shoes, and her earrings. She wedged all these in the shiny purse and slowly approached the grate, twisting her hair up as she walked.

Jen watched her in disgust but turned around when she felt a man's lips on her neck. "Jesus Christ. Get off me."

The man had gotten out of the sewer and was standing with them in the street. Elisia watched him drop her keys into a pocket in his filthy trench coat. Jason stared at the man.

He had fat legs and a skinny face. His eyes were brooding and possessive. Under the paint-stained trench coat he wore two cardigan sweaters, a work shirt, and a hot pink tee shirt full of holes that said *Titty Tahiti Parasails* in garish fluorescent rainbow letters. Green sweat pants covered what looked like old khaki pants. Both pairs of pants were tucked into thick red tube socks which had been repaired more than once, likely by him from the looks of the workmanship. And although on each hip a basketball shoe was tied to a belt loop of the khaki pants, he wore brand new Doc Martens.

"What the fuck do you think you're doing?" Jen could not get away from the man but she yelled right into his pinched red face. "Jason. Are you a fucking idiot? Get this freak away from me."

Elisia looked on as if from a distance thinking, "Nice Christian sentiment, Jen." She lit a cigarette and tried to stand still.

"No harm done, little lady. No harm done. No sense gettin' into a row over this little nothing. Just sayin' hello. Just sayin' hello." He left Jen sitting on the curb and sprang over to Elisia on the sidewalk. "So I'll bet these is your keys, eh? Got another cigarette for a good-lookin' man like me?"

Elisia found him a cigarette and let him light it himself.

He turned the lighter over in his hand several times, assessing its value before handing it back.

Elisia felt defensive. "My dad got me that in Spain."

"Nice dad. That's what I like to see. No more of these absent fathers. Gotta have no kind of respect for a bastard who's so afraid of his own shadow he can't hold a kid on his lap for ten minutes. If he gives you anymore problems, you let me know."

Jen stared at the man. "What are you talking about? Why would anyone let you know?"

The man laughed out loud. He had six or eight teeth left that all seemed in different states of decay. He ended up bent over and coughing. The three of them watched him spit something large in the grass and then he stood up, pointing at Jen, "Just a little fun, lady. Don't you know how to have a little fun? Maybe I do the drugs. But maybe I'm just makin' a little jokey joke. No harm done to you either way and yet look at that face you givin' me." He turned to Elisia, careful not to blow smoke at her. "You see that face."

Elisia had but wasn't sure she wanted to side with the man just yet. "What your name?"

"Name? Does it look like I'm applying for a job here?"

Jason put his hands on his hips and looked up and down the street. He was impatient. He was uncomfortable. He was embarrassed. He was going to be late for soccer.

"What if I told you I ain't got no name? What if I'm a John fucking Doe? Huh? What'd you say to that? You gonna give me grief over that?"

Jen still hadn't stood up and was on the verge of tears.

But Elisia wasn't easily intimidated. "I don't give a shit what your name is. I was just making conversation. So if you want to stand there in that god-awful mess of clothes making philosophical riddles all day, fine. You can have my keys and I can call the cops."

"Oo-ee. Whoa there, little momma." Now he bent down and solicited Jen's sympathy. "She's a bit worked up over nothing, or is it me?" Jen looked at Jason who was beginning to gain strength.

"Look. Nobody's calling the cops. You didn't do anything to us. And all we want is the keys."

"You want keys? Then why you throwin' shit in the gutter? You want something you'd think you'd hold onto it a little tighter. Or not even walk over a grate. The underworld's my home, kid. And in my world it's finders keepers, stealers keepers, and for those that get uppity and bitch a lot, like you doing right now, there ain't many friends."

Elisia suppressed her laughter. Both Jen and Jason had the same self-involved martyr expression on their faces.

Jason's retort was weak, "Underworld?"

The man ignored him and was on the porch. "Are you going to invite me in or don't you want me to cook you three the best dinner you ever gonna eat?" But without time for any of them to choose, the man was in the house rooting through the kitchen. He opened a closet and played with a few things. He took Brillo pads out of the box, juggled them, then held one up to the light and tried to look through it. Tossing the box back on a shelf he took several bottles in a row, opened them, drawing long breaths in through his nose to smell the products. All these were replaced from where they had come. Then he walked all the way into the tiny closet and spent a minute climbing in and out of a mop bucket repeatedly while mumbling what sounded like a children's jump rope chant.

After this was done he assumed a more businesslike demeanor. He put on an apron and went through an elaborate handwashing ritual somewhat like a surgeon and somewhat like a priest before giving communion. The kids stood together out of his way and watched everything.

After forty-five minutes he steered them all to the coffee table in the living room. He turned the TV over on its side and took down a sheet that doubled as curtains. He threw this over the TV and called it a sideboard.

The kids sat on the floor in silence. They all looked from one to the next about to laugh, all ready to call 911 if any of the others suggested it.

The man opened his nylon duffel bag. He fingered through it carefully, holding various objects aloft, considering each in terms of its benefit, beauty, or purpose. After much deliberation whatever decisions needed to be made were made and he began flitting around setting the table in front of them. Each had a newspaper place mat. Each of them had a plate made of Saran Wrap. Each had an empty can as a water glass and a small empty jar for beer, which also came out of the bag.

When it came to flatware each was treated differently. Elisia was given a broken chopstick and a plastic Dairy Queen spoon. Jason had an X-ACTO knife and a tongue depressor, and Jen was provided with a razor blade and three finishing brads. It seemed Jen had the best of the best and the others were graced with the opportunity to share his finery.

Without knowing exactly why, all three of them did feel honored.

A centerpiece was quickly furnished by grabbing things from around the room. It consisted of a baseball trophy draped in Mardi Gras beads standing on a Precious Moments limited edition collectible plate. Five minutes of consultation was devoted to this, the man having Jason turn the plate slowly as he moved quickly from lamp to lamp turning them on or off in various combinations. Finally it was decided that the bat should face the south window and the player himself should look toward the kitchen. The overhead light was turned off, the standing lamp in the corner was turned to the middle setting, and the halogen lamp was at three-quarter strength. When Elisia and Jen suggested that the Venetian blinds should be opened halfway the man kissed them both, proclaiming their absolute genius. It was a simple arrangement, but with the ambient light striking it perfectly it was something close to beautiful.

The man found a radio station playing jazz and began to hum along. None of the kids was breathing. Then in a magnanimous show of creation the man appeared with plates lined up on both arms. These were laid on the TV/sideboard. And then dinner was served.

The top half of a pantyhose egg was used to serve the various delectables. Steamed apple peel, steamed potato with blackberry jam, steamed hot dogs julienne, a small side garnish of cold and heavily-peppered corn mixed with bits of processed American cheese slices, and the apples smashed, steamed, and buttered, covered in soy sauce.

The kids stared at the feast.

Jason began cautiously eating individual pieces of corn with his X-ACTO knife.

Elisia decided to switch her sociology project from "The Modern Day Immigrant" to "Luxuries of the Homeless Life."

And Jen looked toward the man who was leaning in the kitchen doorway drinking a beer. "Aren't you going to join us?"

Shaking his head adamantly, "Couldn't possibly. The chef never eats his own creation."

Elisia raised her eyebrows and stared intently at the baseball trophy to keep from laughing.

But following Jason's valiant lead the girls began to eat.

As they were finishing up and helping the man wash his things and put them back into the bag, he held up a small Salvation Army bell and rang it intermittently.

He put his hand over the bell and leaned toward them in condescending explanation. "My cell phone. I'll be just a minute." He leaned back on his heels assuming that crossed-arm-looking-around stance so many businessmen use on the street. "Yes. Oh, I know. I certainly do understand. If you aren't satisfied with the product we will by all means be willing to negotiate an exchange. No, sir, you should not even think of considering the competition. I back this business with everything I have. You need not worry. You need not worry. You need not worry."

He was crying.

Jason moved toward the telephone just to be ready. The girls stared in fear.

Tossing the bell into the bag he vigorously took Elisia by the shoulders. "I'm so sorry, baby. I'm so sorry. I never meant to let things go this far. I thought I had that contract. I really did. We've still got each other. Don't go. Please don't go. Jesus, don't go. Okay. Okay. But if you really are going take my car. I can't stand to think of you in that old beast of yours." He pressed Elisia's keys into her hand. "No! No, but you can't take her. I'll never see her again. I can't believe this. This isn't us.

Money isn't everything. Money isn't everything. Money isn't everything. Money—"

Quickly and with his voice changing abruptly, he turned to Jason. He took Jason's hand in a firm handshake as though they were closing a deal. "I'm glad you were satisfied. I certainly hope we'll hear from you soon. If you have any problems at all you know to call. We'll have to get back out for some golf as soon as this foul weather breaks." He patted Jason hard on the shoulder and turned to Jen.

He squatted down and kissed her forehead. Then as he stroked her hair and smiled he said in quiet reassuring tones, "I know, baby. You're right. It will be weird. But your mommy knows what's best for all of us. That's why I love her. As much as I like to think I take care of her she takes care of me too. And she'll take care of you too, honey. So be a big girl. And don't worry about Daddy. I'll be fine. I'll be fine. I'll be fine."

The man turned to Elisia and Jason with a finger to his lips implying that the child was asleep. He picked up his bag, careful not to let it rattle. He nodded curtly to Jason and mouthed, "I'll always love you," to Elisia as he backed out the door onto the porch.

Without a word the three left in the room began to put things back in order. Elisia cleaned up the kitchen while Jen and Jason put the TV in the right place and the sheet back over the window. The closet was arranged again. The coffee table was wiped off. The Venetian blinds were closed. Elisia got her things together and got ready to leave. She smiled at Jen. Jen smiled back. They all stood in the living room that still smelled like the sewer. Jason cleared his throat and went to pull the Mardi Gras beads off the trophy.

"Leave them." Jen carefully picked up the plate and placed the centerpiece on top of the television. Elisia opened her cigarette case and pulled one out. She looked at the lighter in her hand and thought vaguely of her father. She moved toward the door and pushed the screen door open. Jen began to cry, and Jason had nothing to say. But then Elisia came back in for a second and reaching toward the TV she turned the little plate slightly so that the man on the trophy faced the kitchen and his bat was pointed toward the south window.

Sometimes love comes easily. And other times love comes so hard there is nothing left of you.

NEWLYWEDS

"Listen to this."

"Oh God, come on. No more of that bullshit."

"Just one."

"I'm tired. Why are you always trying to get better at everything? Just let it go." Electricity cost a lot. So they tried not to use the dryer much. He sat next to the pile of clean laundry on the couch. Faded colors were stacked on the bottom and strewn around his head were light colored towels that fought the humidity and pretended to dry. His boots were near the door and his feet were buried in a bright pile of plastic. Children's toys. "I swear that librarian must be damn sick of looking at you every day."

She laughed and stood up. "No more than I am of you." She looked at the dishes and bottles in the sink and then turned her attention back to the television. Her hair was weak and hid behind her ears sheepishly. She moved around the small room, waiting.

He tried again. "So what do you think about this weekend?"

She looked at cans of pasta. Her mother never served pasta from a can. She looked at the vegetables and the tiny jars of baby food. She held onto a little gold cross on a necklace. She pulled it from one side of her neck to the other. She held in her mouth and rubbed it over her lips absently.

Shutting the cabinet she said, "I can think of better things to do than listen to your brothers talk about their cars and sports and all their other bullshit."

He flipped channels. Passed the news. Passed the evangelists. Slowed at a cartoon and landed on a special about Siamese twins.

DRESS UP

The engineer (and his girlfriend)
walking head tilted away
self-conscious and a tube of yellow
plans in the left hand (her glove in his
right) rush down
a paved alley wasting youth in a
hurried game of dress up.
But just another of the bubbles she keeps
up and can't wait
for twenty years of looking
out a kitchen window, hoping
the diamond won't get washed
down a drain. But I can't deny
how happy he seems or that
she has him this morning
at 7:37 clenched in her own
plans with a left gloved
"Good morning, honey" hand.

I wish I had someone to watch me get undressed.

JUST SO

Sometimes as a child I was left in the library of Saint Joseph's College. I never read much but I wandered through the old, still stacks smelling the paper die. I climbed on the radiators, sometimes burning the insides of skinny legs to sit in a window and watch the trees let go their leaves.

On brave days I eased myself down a steep flight of stairs and looked at art books in the orange half-light, scared of the studying students. But almost every time, after I had looked up my birth announcement from *The Republican* on microfilm, I would go find Jodi or Mr. V. and ask to be let into the record room.

A smile, and the librarian would finish with the stamping or rubber bands around cards or checking out a student or phone call question. Then the slowish figure would move back to a desk or an office in order to find a set of keys that seemed too loud for a library.

And I followed the swinging skirt or the skinny pants, always watching the tile change in diamonds from black to maroon and back again and again. Until the light swept up an old wooden floor and crossed us over onto gray hard linoleum. And the keys would come. "Maybe this one. No, let's try it with the longer one." Or, "Maybe I grabbed the wrong set."

When the dark door opened past the groove in the floor a room sat up drearily and welcomed us for a visit. (Even though it would rather not have.) Two windows for light and wall shelves made for display. "Pick anything you would like to listen to, dear. We will find it." Patiently.

But I always chose the same thing. I never wanted music. And I never wanted too much yesterday laughter. So we found the place where I saw what I needed and used the chair to reach it again.

Rudyard Kipling's *Just So Stories*. I guess, now, I could blame him for his faults as a man or for teaching me that very European empirical morality that determines so much of my worldview. But at the time, the LP sat thin in its bright orange package and always remembered me. Even when I had been out to play every day for the summer or hadn't seen it for a winter of school. The librarian's special walking away after the locked-up door. Trusting me and confident I knew the players well.

I pulled at an edge of the wooden room and sat down amidst the thick blond lacquer with my chest close enough to the table. The record came out and went spinning away. The headphones were turquoise and plastic and old. They fell sometimes. Too big for me, but they could usually be conned into place.

And the voice began always the same with, "On the sea, once upon a time, O my Best Beloved, there was a Whale, and he ate fishes. He ate the starfish and the garfish, and the crab and the dab, and the plaice and the dace, and the skate and his mate, and the mackerel and the pickereel, and the really truly twirly-whirly eel."

That voice. Deep and buoyed by the daddies of the world stretching strong arms between each rhyme. Laughing, almost, all the time. And keeping you caught in that almost-fallen-asleep-but-still-have-to-listen place. My legs gone swinging under the table, and my elbows turning red from the weight of my head in my growing up hands, leaning with the headphones toward the voice. Pressing him closer into my world. Always divided from the needle scratching on the record, around, and around, and around.

The stories spun on. And the voice followed suit. And I lay my head on the cool table—just to look out the window for a while. "And the Parsee lived by the Red Sea with nothing but his hat and his knife and a cooking-stove of the kind that you must particularly never touch." The tree shadows reached down and whispered their hushes to me from the ceiling, then the walls, then the floor, and out again leaving behind their indigo gossip. "The suspenders were left behind, you see, to tie the grating with; and that is the end of that tale." My legs cold in the dark blue evening curled against the hard arms of the chair looking for somebody's lap.

"Once upon a most early time was a Neolithic man. He was not a Jute or an Angle, or even a Dravidian, which he might well have been, Best Beloved, but never mind why. He was a Primitive, and he lived cavily in a Cave, and he wore very few clothes, and he couldn't read and he couldn't write and he didn't want to, and except when he was hungry he was quite happy. His name was Tegumai Bobsulai, and that means, 'Man-who-does-not-put-his-foot-forward-in-a-hurry;' but we, O Best Beloved, will call him Tegumai for short."

And then the sleep came until Mom was finished with her music or Dad had cleaned up the lab.

NEW ORLEANS SIDEWALK

I took the dog and walked down the street toward Bob Dylan's house in order to see his flowers. I took my camera I suppose as an afterthought, but nonetheless I did take my camera. Standing there among the old oak roots, where the dog seemed eager to stop, in front of the fence of security cameras defining a great man's perimeter, I wondered at the huge banks of white azaleas. Six feet tall and more wide than that. Sun on each but cool stone still on the porch. And I wondered what Bob Dylan looks like or what songs he sings and could not fill my mind with acceptable answers. The place was for sale apparently and my friends couldn't be sure that Bob Dylan really ever lived there.

The pictures aren't very good. If the azaleas look good you can't see the house. If the house is included it seems to converge at its roof. And none of these images show the beauty of that endless green lawn, so rare in a city of that size. And the quality of the photos was not improved by the simultaneous facts that I was standing on broken slabs of the sidewalk, being yanked by a dog leash, and wedging my camera through the cast iron fence.

After that, I was glad not to worry with the bother of Bob Dylan's house anymore. I walked on down to the cemetery and let the dog jump at spiders in the tall grass. I walked down to the river staging this or that version of Mark Twain, Jeff Buckley, and the slow tankers' working men still.

I liked the lady in a bright white shirt walking too fast with a piece of pizza smothered in grease.

HE PROPOSED AND THEN

Him: Just tell me. I'm always supposed to know what to do when you don't tell me shit.

Her: Like you don't know.

Him: I don't.

Her: Then you're blind.

Him: Don't be condescending to me.

Her: Don't be a martyr.

Him: Whatever.

Her: Do you know what women are?

Him: What? What kind of question is that? You think I'm going to answer that?

Her: Do you know what women are?

Him: They're people.

Her: But do you know what they are?

Him: Are you going to get all fucked up and philosophical on me again? Because I'm sick of it. I don't want to hear all this bullshit.

Her: Exactly.

Him: Fuck you.

Her: Don't you walk away from me.

Him: Fine.

Her: Fine.

Him: Tell me about women. Who are they? Get on your feminist high-horse. Shit, tell me you're a lesbian. I really don't care at this point. I don't give a fuck anymore because this isn't love. I don't know what you do to me but it isn't love. It's degenerate. You're a fucking infection.

Her: Nice.

Him: No. No, I don't care. I'm sick of being nice just because I'm supposed to be. You can say whatever you want and I'm just supposed to take it. But I am done. So go ahead. Tell me all about what women are, because it's as good a way to waste my time with chaos.

She looks at him. He is red and shaking, helpless with misunderstanding. She flinches and takes a deep breath in spite of his pain.

Her: Chaos?

He looks at her and waits.

Her: Chaos is okay. It's more natural than any of your world. It is the only natural irretrievable progression. It's okay. And we aren't wasting our time. Or at least I'm not wasting mine. This is just what Wall Street uses to control the world and it is TV and it is classes and work. It is not rocks, Babe. It's not mountains or clouds.

He is laughing and sits down on a cement bench. She kneels in front of him and holds his hands. He protects her with his knees around her shoulders.

Him: So tell me about women. They're mountains and clouds?

Her: Are you sure you want to hear this?

Him: Yeah.

Her: Well, I'm not a feminist or a lesbian, and I'll tell you why those ideas are too simplistic. Good for somebody. Sure. They run counter to society. Yes, there is a male patriarchy, but fuck that. Women are subject to men, but they aren't just women either. They are half from woman and half from man.

Him: So are men.

Her: No. Not really. Each man starts new. Each man is additive. He is his father and his mother: XY. But women are their mother and their father's mother: XX.

Him: When was the last time you took biology?

Her: Just listen. In men, XY each is from the identity of his own parents. The chromosomes came from their ancestors and yes, they're mutating and all that but the identity a man receives is as alive as his mother and father at the time of conception. That was his dad's Y. And that X was his mom's.

Him: Barr bodies? Have you—

Her: Don't push me. Men are additive. They are always approaching infinity. But women are pulled back from the present. They are removed from infinity because they are the consummation of the mother and the identity the father's mother gave to her son, which was then sacrificed for his own identity.

Him: It's part of his identity.

Her: I'm not done. So as man is built, man upon man, as if every one is an extension of Adam and each based in God—or if you don't want to use God, then each benefits from the ability to plant his identity in an unbroken line of men. But women. Women are built on a fault line. Women are founded on what men can live without. Adam was fine missing a rib and yet it was Eve's creation. Or again getting God stuff out, women are made from the half of identity men choose not to pursue.

Him: Nobody chooses anything.

Her: In a way. Yet isn't it true they do?

He tries to respond but is tired. And confused. And just hoping she could be happier. It is hard for him to process everything. She goes on.

Her: So you—you're a man. You are your mom and dad fucking. Maybe it wasn't love, but it could have been and even if it wasn't it is based in the present. It is action. It is passion. Men are created in that heat. They are forged in orgasm.

Him: Have you been reading poetry again? Or did your sister send you another one of those tapes? This is ridiculous. Women are the same as guys.

Her: Just listen. Women are very similar, it's true. So similar in fact that virtually no one sees the implications of the nuances and so they account their pain to inferiority, insecurity, or whatever. But don't you see? A woman is made from her mom fucking her father's mom. It's sick. It's an impossibility. It's based in decay.

Him: This is fucking crazy.

Her: Two more minutes. If the man has X and Y but suppresses X all those years and lives in Y then when a girl is conceived that X is only his mother lying on her back however many years before. That X is what the father mounted. That X was last thought of when those grandparents fucked that father into being. That X is another rejection, because the father goes on being a man. If a boy is conceived that is the love and passion a man has for a woman.

Him: Can you be a little more abstract?

Her: But if a girl is conceived that is the hatred between the mother and the mother-in-law. That is the tension of like forces in proximity. Like magnets. That's her. And those Xs have been passed down for however many hundred years in that disjunct fashion. All Xs eventually having that poison about them. Not like the Ys, which hold that solid background.

So women grow up with this at the core of their being. So it comes to nights like this between you and me. It comes down to these fights. It comes down to house payments and colors for cars and children's schools and names for the dog. It comes into every decision. That blackness of all those Xs. And the man—each with his Y from God—always wins.

So he is able to be silent and proud, unforgiving, focused, and feels no understanding for the chaotic world. Woman is different. She stands shadowed by her mundane life. Hoping her children are good enough for the fucked-up world. Hoping to catch some sun on her face from a deep damned canyon wedged between two monstrous obsidian cliffs. But never really believing in herself and her beliefs. Never content and constantly questioning her limits. Not expanding them but assuring herself as to where they are because they are constants. They are her means of support.

She's tired and frail and she knows better than to divest herself of the limits the way a submarine knows not to crack its walls. So here I am tonight with you asking me to marry you. And all I can think of is your mother.

All I can think is that you should be happy and that the world should go on as it has always gone on. What right have I to go off alone? I have no right. My duty is to you and your love for me. My duty is to that diamond—right?—and to the three-year-old in a grocery cart that comes with it. Why is that my duty? Not because of you. Not even because of society. Because you don't care. And they don't care. No matter what I do—whether I hold up a feminist label or wave a rainbow flag—they'll see the diamond ring and the grocery cart. So that's not it.

But I have this duty to my mother.

I'm supposed to endure what she endured to show I'm not too good for her. To show that I appreciate all she's done for me and believe that all her pain, which she has stuck down in that dark cavern, was not for no reason. That's why she calls and asks if I have a boyfriend. That's why she's always pressuring me to get married. That's why she'll think I've failed no matter what else I do, if I don't have kids. And even if I was with you, Babe. Even with you. I love you. I know it would work. I know I would love our kids. I know I could spend the rest of my life with your voice and your arms and your eyes. I know that. But why? Why? Because no matter how liberal or equal or nontraditional a relationship we create, I will still disappear. I will still become that thing that is caught between my duty to my mother and my love for you.

That's what marriage is and the rest gets squeezed out. The rest is a hobby. The rest is a part-time job at the deli. Or it's the doctor's nurse. Whatever. Look at it. The feminists cut off one side of the canyon—their duty to their mother. And lesbians cut off the other—their love for a man.

But what is that?

Steeped so long in what all I've just said, without replacing those barriers with another of the same magnitude— like social isolation, hatred, contempt, or artistry—that woman is bound to dribble away. And if she is not taken for insane, she is only a thin film with her cohesive force, her memories of self from childhood.

Even so. It is time that is the enemy. If a woman can remove one side of the canyon, love for a man or duty to the mother, and stop time simultaneously, then she is preserved. She would be tall and stand like a sculpture formed from the mold of her mind. The beauty of her vision of the future—the part of her that would correspond to the pressure of her love for one man—on one side. And on the other, the side that affronted her duty for her mother, would be her integrity, responsibility, and perception of the past. It would be her. Frozen there and beautiful.

He wants to kiss her. And he wants to run. He tilts his head back toward the sky and wishes she could relax or trust him or see what he sees. Tears flood his eyes and the stars swim past and away so as not to be intrusive. He blinks several times and stands up. She fidgets and wants him to talk. She doesn't want him to be hurt. She just wants him to understand.

Him: I love you. And that's not going to change. I knew you needed more from me and I thought that meant marriage.

He looks at her. Her face is blank and her body inert.

Him: But if more is realizing I'm a mold or a barrier or Y or whatever and I've got to go—I don't know. Shit. I—

She laughs.

Her: Don't get all deep on me, Babe. You want to make me cry?

He laughs and shakes his head. But yes. He wants her to cry. Other girls would cry. He wants her to wear the stupid ring and be happy. He wants her to have everything. He wants her to understand.

Him: God damn it. All I want to know is do you want this fucking ring? Because if you don't, I can take it back and buy a motorcycle.

Her: Oh. Yeah. Please buy a motorcycle. I love all those songs about motorcycles. Would you take me for rides, Babe?

He closes the little black velvet box around the ring and shoves it in his pocket. He picks her up and throws her over his shoulder.

Him: Fuck the motorcycle. I'll take you for a ride right now.

She stops him, puts her hands on his chest, and looks him in the eye. Her: I just don't want to have kids. I'm worried I'll fuck it up. That they'll fuck me up.

Him: Okay. Why didn't you just say that?

Her: I didn't know how. It doesn't seem like something you're supposed to say.

Him: Supposed to say to who? Fuck it. It's just me.

He kisses her on the hip and climbs over the railing. The lights are orange over the water and the sky is close. He looks at the moon, that half-moon that you always wish were more poetic, and jumps into the river, letting her laugh and scream and cling to him all the way down.

SAD ASIAN FACE

Sad Asian face

in a trench coat alley

letting the snow go

all around his

thinning uncovered head.

Warm brown face

in an altogether

huge gray world.

Letting looks go

too often towards

the pavement and

opening his closing

gloved fists repeatedly

against the cold

professorial thoughts.

MONDAY NIGHT RAIN WITH FOOTBALL

The room was really too small for the size of all the men on the television. Like looking through a child's dollhouse window: valiant Patriots and runaway Dolphins came through the screen to us sweaty, and heaving.

A fat Christmas tree wore a single ornament in the way a poor girl might wear a silver chain. It must have been a gift. The talk was small, filled with *I remembers* and the *Well if I was hims*.

We all drank beer. Lots of beer and the short guy and his sister seemed to fight with the giants in the window for our attention.

I would have left hours before if it hadn't been raining.

YOU'RE SIERRA LEONE

You're Sierra Leone. But just a child hiding out. Did you know there is a cottonwood tree here, too, young sir? Mine stands with roots tangled in dark Indiana soil, leaning over a river made simply when a strand of God's hair touched the earth by accident. It's in the little ravine behind my house where the vulture likes to swoop-beat slow and rise again on warmer air. I've known that tree my entire life. With its shivering leaves and its snow tears. Charming. Peaceful. My constant refuge of hide-and-seek.

And now, God, now, I hear about your cottonwood tree. On its red soil. Where you must be afraid even of its immutable peace. Because the leaves are your only witnesses. Irretrievable when they fall.

Can it be possible? Who is stopped listening to that? Can the world be so cruel? I had hoped not. But there you were, finding God's grace in a plane full of bombs. Saved from your own execution by so many others. And now these photographs. Coming to me between ads for push-up bras and cellulite cream in some *Vanity Fair.*

These photographs of soldiers wearing blue flip-flops with their camouflage garb. Where bloody smiles point victoriously to severed heads. Where the man from Chicago, the good doctor who wanted to return for his family, lies watching death approach as if on a beach gazing at the gulls pass. He knows. He knew what I wonder. Who are these fucking murderers?

You wanted to explain. So you began with your careful midnight matchsticks. Huddled close. Writing with lime juice ink. Waiting for someone to wet your autobiography with their own tears so as to be able to read it.

But as you come running from the bombs with your new cache of these horrid photographs and you huddle with the cottonwood which shudders itself in fear, whom do you meet? Are you looking for an accomplice? I only know how to play. Are you looking for help? I am only a child on a river bank. And if you are looking for someone who understands your hideous fear I am not afraid—don't have to be. What would I fear in my cottonwood? I am only hiding from a friend. And you, oh God, you are hiding from the same kind of immortal accident that made my hairline river. From his shifting feet or leaning elbow. Trying to anticipate his tired movements so as to avoid his weight.

God is careless, I recognize.

And I begin to cry. You look at me, scared. Realizing that we're not hiding together. That your photographs can only be part of my game. I scream at you in my own defense, "Look! Look where your pictures are! Look what else came with them! Movie stars? Technology moguls! Shiny pages and pretty colors!" And I'm so sorry. In a thousand ways. Because if it weren't for the movies, I never would have known. And if I never had known, maybe your God behind the cottonwood has no purpose.

But now what? So many barriers between us keeping me from understanding or helping or from just giving you hand-holding hope behind that tree while you wait. Divisive realities.

It's hard to be friends sometimes.

So now here we are together for a moment behind our cottonwood trees, one on each side of the world, one on each side of twenty years. And all I can offer, all I can give you, is that I know what it feels like to be waiting there. Those moments under the cottonwood tree where the leaves chop sunlight into rain. And the wind having fought his way through the chatty leaves reaches your skin simply as a sigh-puff.

To be there quiet. To be there alone.

I know that, young sir.

But I will not wish to share your anguish. Ever. Or to be hiding in that bloody kind of soil. And I don't know what to do, now. With these pictures on my late-night bed. You are gone, now. I suppose. And the cottonwood leaves have fallen.

PAY DAY

She sat with her shoulders forward. Slumped over her too-expensive food and listened to her fate sitting at a table nearby.

She may never have noticed them. But when you are eating alone, even in an expensive and luxurious restaurant, people tend to steal your space. They know you have no real reason to defend it: you without your anyone who wants to come for dinner. And so they come up from behind your chair. They take the space you cannot catch. The space you cannot see. And because this is the place they are intent on taking, you shiver and recoil from their proximity.

The girl sat rigid and the woman, deep in a discussion with her friend, leaned into that most precious space. Threw her coat on top of the girl with a curt meaningless apology. And insisted throughout the night on causing the backs of their chairs to click together but only once in a while. Like water torture. Or the way clouds slow down when you are planning their route across the sun.

The woman explained life to the girl. Talking a little too loudly. Insisting that she hear. Jealous of her thin wrists. Even more envious of her naked face and hands. Their drifting voices told the girl: College would fade. She would be fat. She would have kids who hated her. She would want to cry for no reason on the most beautiful days. That's what they said, but even so the girl sat alone, treating herself to a dinner too big for her paycheck. It would have been nice: the thick old carpet, the crystal, the soft thin beef. But instead she was alone and unable to escape eavesdropping on the middle-aged women behind her.

From across the table and faded blond, "Well, wasn't it just the funniest. How we have changed since then. I can't believe such a young life could possibly exist in anyone's heart anymore. Can you?"

The first tilting her head and smiling piteously with only a hairsbreadth between the back of the girl's chair and her own, "Of course not." And with her neatly folded peacock tail napkin she cleaned the sides of her smirk with affected blots and dabs. She must have thought that rich people would approve. She must have wanted to be rich. She must have hoped someone was watching. After thinking too long and with no reason to say it, "Crib sheets have taken on a completely different meaning, haven't they?"

It was sort of funny. Funny to think of women cheating the world with their over-and-over bassinet babies. Soggy morals and too little time to think of something better to say. But the other woman didn't understand. She had cheated too much in school and done way too much baby doll laundry to hear a connection so maddening.

It was inescapable. The regular women dressed up in their going-out clothes. One with tacky lipstick. The other a country girl from New Hampshire. Only because she kept saying, with a condescending laugh packed between her cheeks like cotton or a bite too big to taste, "You know me, dear, just a simple country girl from New Hampshire."

And the other laughed the same cotton laugh and pretended to relate. She did relate of course, she had to, but never really admitted how similar they were. Never really allowed herself to be the same. And so the laugh was pretend, even though it shouldn't have been. (You know what I mean. They're everywhere.)

And so the girl waited. Trying not to chew. Sucking on her salad. Her fork elbow glued to her ribs. The waitress was late to be somewhere else so the girl didn't ask for ice cream. And when she stood up her chair knocked against the older woman's shoulder.

The woman spun on the girl and stared hard into the young eyes silently with her scolding, "College will fade. You will be fat. You will have kids who hate you. You will want to cry for no reason on the most beautiful days. You will never learn to paint or act or be able to get into the best places. You will have to wash and feed the dog. You will never be thanked. You will have to give away your beauty to someone more deserving." That's what they said, those middle-aged eyes.

And the girls stared back, "Perhaps, but maybe I am not as weak as you. Maybe I will be glad to do it. Maybe I'll always enjoy eating alone and I won't have to meet friends I don't care about. Maybe I'll be kind enough to appreciate a world that gave me constant change."

Screaming eyes. Hateful and strong. Only for a second though. The waitress at the next table over only had time to pour half a glass of water and laugh with her, "No ice please" customer.

And the girl, having bumped the woman's shoulder, and insisting on overcoming whatever it was that made them the same, smiled and touched the selfish woman's arm. "Excuse me, ma'am. I didn't realize you were there." So close.

The woman looked away and hid her shoulders in the hollow of her Sunday coat. The other woman sucked her salad. No one can really afford a manicure. Careless spending.

Needless expense. It would have been nice though, thick old carpet, the crystal, the soft thin beef.

Intellect is Imagination waking in adulthood.

THE SOUND'S EDGE

Here they are again: baby clams with pink, purple, and orange quarter-inch personalities. They're not all alive. Piles of tiny clam shells extend down below your feet in a cloud-colored shimmer given by some two-inch wash of the water. In a handful most are still alive, going on with the work of tickling skin. Some are newly crushed, learning a strange kind of dying, bloodless and slippery, thrust between curious fingers not quite wanting to help. But then those few. Past it all already. Tiny death leaves. Pairs of angel wings. And the tiny deaths leave pairs of angels' wings. No mamas laughing at memories and no reason to follow the tide. But such a beautiful tossing tomb there, two inches under the waves' own kiss goodbye.

RIVERHEAD

I know that a garden has died. Caught tight by a country road someone insisted on paving so the chickens forgot to come home for the ax and scald, the feathers plucked and then that potato field covered in sod long after the fourth child (quiet and chewing fast) knew she was the runt of their not-enough-for-dinner fish porches.

I know that garden has died. Caught too fast by hungry water eating its way through the cliff and up under the house where a lemon yellow rowboat—named a dead sister—sleeps upside-down in the sand under a little ark, by the red broken heart wheelbarrow, handles sideways, and sandy cool.

Fishing line wind chimes hang dead-tired of winter waiting for the doors to unlock.

But a garden has died. Forgotten in the sun, like the blue-lidded bag of clothespins turned brittle (and the horseshoe crab) with the mildew and must; and the flag does nothing about screens lifting away from frames fraying, wire by wire, like family.

A garden has died downed with the black cherry corpse of the hurricane season. No one's watching the Rose of Sharon trying to hide in tall grass whispers left by an inattentive scythe, rusting in a shed, which needs to be painted, desperately.

I know that a garden has died.

LINGERIE HANGERS

I found another flaw in our culture. Hangers. Especially hangers in the lingerie section of any major department store. Not hangers in lingerie stores, because they are specialized enough to have nice ribbony hangers with brass knobs to hold things in place. But in department stores, where everyone is supposedly accommodated with one fashion or another all in one place, there is simply not enough room for fancy, wide, ribbony hangers. This leads to a sad state of affairs.

There is a very good reason why you sometimes find bras along the side of the road. Take for instance this afternoon. After shopping for some time I was in a state with which you are all probably familiar. My hair was all staticky from pulling my shirt over my head so many times. I was too hot. I was hungry. I might have had to go to the bathroom. The fluorescent lights were making me vaguely ill, and both of my hands were going to sleep as a result of having so many heavy plastic bags hanging from my wrists.

Then I remembered I needed a bra.

Fine.

So of course being a rather small person with not much to offer in terms of business for the lingerie department, my size was on the lowest rack, very near the floor. I squatted down among my shopping bags and pushed my glasses up with my shoulder.

Women are so enmeshed with retailers in a wrangle for self-esteem that the sizes on underwear are nebulous to the point of meaning nothing. God forbid a tag state the obvious. The retailers stick up pictures of tan, elongated, windblown underwear models and then try to appease every woman's wallet by assuring her she is one of them. This is accomplished through the use of this tag-code, which like any good tool of sabotage is constantly changing. And with all the crash diets, exercise schemes, and preggers/postpartum expansion and contraction women's bodies are changing equally as much.

The bra-tag code is based in a sort of reality: chest measurement and cup size. But the thought that this is in any way a determination of oneself and a tool used to quickly move through the merchandise towards what is most adequate, to say nothing of what may be desirable, is a farce. Then there are the countless added variables, like cute heart-shaped clasp-in-front rhinestone closures with bows glued on or racy tiger stripes rendered in twelve shades of hot pink.

Whether or not the bow will probably come off in the first wash or the hot pink tiger stripes will show through even the most dowdy turtleneck and cardigan, let's leave out preference altogether. Let us focus on need.

A woman approaches a rack looking for a bra. Not a bra for a date. A regular bra to wear to school, work, and whatever community event to which she's promised to devote much too much of her time. She gets caught (by her coat, her kids' coats, her purse, her shopping bags, and her child's hand, all of which she is holding) on every rack of teddies and negligees, which establishes the initial self-consciousness. Regardless of whether she is a woman who wears complex and deviant underclothes or is a woman so put off by the thought that she refuses to look at her four-year-old son for three days after he pulled the crotch of a black velvet hi-cut brief like a slingshot and flipped it into the aisle, seeing teddies and being engulfed by their insinuations of pleasure and one's inevitable lack of ability to live up to such fantasies run totally counter to trying to replace a bra which has begun to fray along the top, needs a safety pin to keep the strap on, or has bent its hooks in the back making it dangerously subject to springing off and discharging its contents at inopportune times.

So after making it past the frilly sea-foam green and black things into the actual realm of bras in a rainbow of what are supposedly flesh tones, she must make another set of decisions. Now I hate to be the bearer of bad news but the fact is, women will never be liberated. Who has the time? Brand, color, strapless, cutest, wide strap, demi-cup, mastectomy, skinny strap, cheap and trashy, things that do a bra's job but aren't really anything at all except hooker uniforms, lacy, racer-back, refined, stretchy, front clasp, push-up, print, see-through, over-priced, grandma industrial strength, elegant, padded, cartoon character, cotton, synthetic, mesh, elegant, athletic, striped, underwire, handmade, miracle, nursing, etc. You might think that some of these decisions are not necessary to make.

Since I am without children you would laugh at my mentioning the nursing bras, but it is absolutely essential that a woman be on the lookout for the bras that she does not want. These antagonists have a way of ending up on the counter with the other bras and looking very normal until one gets home, loses the receipt, has only dirty or wet laundry, and tries to put them on. You can surely imagine how bizarre it might feel to be sitting in an eighth grade history class trying not to draw any testosterone-riddled attention as one tugs at the snaps and zippers in the cups of an inappropriately-purchased brassiere. However, it is my theory that it is because of such mistakes that women learn to feel any level of comfort at all when wearing the teddies and such with their zippers and snaps and inappropriately-placed everything.

There is no sense in getting attached to a comfortable, regular, dependable bra. It is an impossibility for one to replace bras because they do not ever make the same bra twice. Even if they did the little tags that come on the dainty industrial bras are printed with fadeable ink so that once the thing is washed the first time its identity can never again be ascertained.

Then we come back to the hangers. My hands are turning purple with lack of circulation but I am focused and squatting there on the carpet among the thousand brands, colors, styles, etc. And I can't remember what is at home already in the ridiculously full top drawer. (I say ridiculous because although one wears only three or four of the twenty-some bras one owns, the mistakenly-purchased weird bras providing the bulk in number, one can never throw away bras that are perpetually new because they are so damn expensive.) I can't ever remember my size. And even if I did it would be different because of the brand and the amount of elastic and the length of the straps and the size of the cups and everything else.

So I look over at the child who is pulling a magenta satin thong over his head while his mother intentionally ignores him by focusing on a pair of tummy-control hot pants and without another thought plunge my hand into the rack.

It wouldn't matter what I pulled out. I would have bought anything. I really would have. But like a fish caught in a net suddenly I realize I am bound irrevocably among the hangers. They are little brittle straight-across hangers with claws. My hand is bound among them with my shopping bag and there are bra straps entangling my arm and reaching toward my throat with malice. The little boy throws the thong on the floor and runs away in terror, and I am left thrashing on the floor trying to free myself and my chosen merchandise, if at all possible, from the bewildering strands of elastic.

And then of course she appears. "Looking for anything in particular today or just browsing? If you need any help just let me know. My name's Lyona." Then she's gone. The only reason she said her name was because she works on commission. There is no way that she is going to endanger herself amid the hangers on my behalf.

So I fight my way free and leave the store trying not to cry. In the car I am thinking that if the hangers were better, or if they could employ some sort of display like a tool rack or poster file that they would sell a million more bras and the damn things wouldn't be so expensive. Satisfied with my justification I take a deep breath and of course feel a hook flick against my shirt and am driving on the Interstate with an insipid bra crawling around sickly-useless inside my shirt.

135

FIGHTERS

It's 4:44 a.m. and I'm up for the day thanks to the first fight of the year. I live near a rowdy campus bar and there were three guys screaming in the lot behind my house at 4:02. Two on the ground, then three. One screaming, "Let's not do this. We'll all get arrested." The other, "Bring it on, you fucking pussy-man." And the third. "Mike, I'm not going to fight you."

And so it went on until 4:13. Back and forth. And I was afraid from my window, wondering whether someone would get hurt, and if I'd feel guilty for not calling the cops. But one of the guys was my neighbor. So I held off.

By 4:17 the voices had begun to recede somewhere away down the alley. But within three minutes they were growing again. The fighter had turned on the other friend who had been trying to prevent it all. And they were walking fast with beer cans when the cops pulled up in the alley. Guns drawn and everything. Fine. Someone else had called. So talking and talking and talking. Explanation. And I heard the tall one say, "I didn't do a thing." Pussy.

Last year there was a big old huge fight. It woke me up, and I lay in bed pissed off and tired. I finally decided to call the cops. (I've never called the cops except to ask rather obscene things. That was before caller ID. And that was usually from a friend's house anyway.) But when I went to the window to see what was going on three or four cop cars were already there. They were the ones fighting. And the guys they were fighting were black.

One of the black kids (are college kids men?) was bent over a muddy puddle screaming, "My eyes. You fucking sprayed my eyes." And another three were frozen on the porch saying, "This wouldn't happen if we weren't black." One had run away. Two careful white cops and a tall clean-cut black man, who didn't look like a fighter, dressed in a very white sweater, were talking carefully and trying to appease one another. It didn't matter. I saw five black guys get arrested that night. Or at least they all went away in the car.

The white kids tonight weren't screaming at the cops. They didn't mind getting into the car, didn't try to run. But they didn't have to. At 4:42 one of the cops, his gun very nicely stowed away, went into my neighbor's apartment. He was not going to incriminate him. Instead, he turned off the light in the kitchen, found the keys in the bedroom, and came out locking the door up tight, taking care to shut the screen door.

CIARA E.

- 29 September 2000

One eye sky and

one eye sleep. And

three months, day

by new. Your

one eye sky and

one eye sleep

and both Lake

Michigan blue.

AFTER HOURS

I wish you could wander back into the same familiarland where quiet voices recur in chorus. But somehow like lying in bed as a child hearing the TV or Mom on the phone or Dad discussing something in the next room, those separated voices are the best lullaby. Because they mean you are not alone. Such a beautiful shiny restaurant bar. And so much darkness was reassuring. Similar but not the same as the darkness in my apartment after a cocktail party for the wind.

Memories are fickle things. And I suppose a degree of truth is necessary. But I feel that if I am going to have memories at all that they should be beautiful, and so I will tell you this one in that light.

Two years ago I sat on the floor of my silent apartment watching the streetlight and the wind turn my room into a burnt-shadow cocktail party. We chatted, the shadows and I, about the weather, the night sky, and while the walls weren't listening I told the most attractive shadow quiet whisper stories. I've never seen the moon so drunk. And the shadows and I were embarrassed for him. We were glad when he left. But it seemed, as soon as the clouds appeared, the streetlight had other plans. And I saw him later rushing madly through that canopy not caring a bit that I could see just about everything. I was so tired by the time the wind threw down an almost-finished cigarette and let the shadows on his arm wave good-bye.

I hate to clean up after a party. Too many barely-made memories.

I decided to leave the cleaning to the cat. And as she licked the crystal carefully and lightly stepped among the plates, assessing them each with a sniff, I curled what was left of the oh-so-good party feeling up under my legs and began my mind retreat. Sometimes I do that, and in a memory, I craved mangoes and sweet sticky rice.

There was a bar in Texas. Really it was a Thai restaurant, but the shiny black bar with neon lights and glass brick stretched out comfortably between the tables. I used to go with my friend late at night. So late the place was just a neon sign advertising to no one. Three rooms of luxurious red chairs stripped of their grandeur in the dark. The space filling up behind and under everything with the cool blue light around the bar.

We never got there before they closed, but we pounded like fools until we made friends with the tired cooks who didn't feel like opening the door. We would get the last of the sticky rice, some drinks, and mangoes. We ate listening to women who had loosened their embroidered silk dresses speak Thai. We watched the men in tuxedos with their feet up smoking and staring at reruns of soccer on TV. There was never any money on those nights. No one cared by that time. Just wanted a little time to chat and laugh and allow the evening to dissipate.

ANTHEM

"Oh, say can you see,

by the dawn's early light,"

rush hour traffic stopped in the

fair lanes of their everyday expedition?

Couped up behind mercury windows

with a bottle of sable polish

for the longest talon or tercel,

they mark vii ways to

achieva better life. Greener grass.

And just ahead of the neighbors

on their slow morning way

to the metro,

"What so proudly we hailed"

Le Baron Ford caravans from their

commercial Monte Carlo ease.

Billboard magazines. Flipping

through Sirius radio stations.

that jam the blazer
and Avalon's unstoppable
push toward the Yukon.

A prairie highway whispers fast
as the beetles venture home
"at the twilight's last gleaming."
When their civic accord returns
once more to the town and country.
Slow and fast.

"Whose broad stripes" define fields
of plenty? "And bright stars" blanch
the sodium night? Whose streetlights
and trash along endless fence lines?
Whose telephone-pole rivers
and oven-hot asphalt are ever
gonna end?

And can they have heard Lincoln's
freeway "through the perilous fight"
while explorers, rangers,
Cherokees, and sidekicks
(Zero to sixty. Seventy-five. Eighty.)
play samurai games with cutlass sabers?

Passing and braking, passing again
with a just-in-case Beretta hidden
under the seat?

"O'er the ramparts we watched"
for El Dorado and the sterling hope
prelude to an odyssey dream of
suburban worlds. The regal citations.
A century-long mirage, and fantasy
glimpses of the neon sundance
with infinity, looking for clover-leaves,
and charging ahead like a lynx.

Every night on the double-
line contours the windstar,
skylark, and Taurus danced high,
"so gallantly streaming." Bright
white lumina entered the tollway gate.

And from that prism a grand prix
spectrum, of "the rockets'
red glare" broke. Such light
of the aurora sky rests
quick on two beating
firebird wings. Thunder

and a semi crash.

I watched the grand am probe
Montana, and saw "the bombs
bursting in air." The roadrunners
drive the mountains flat
and bridge the sea highway
with a tempo unbroken by night
or day. And the maxima traffic
moves faster and faster toward free.
Who can believe
there is anywhere not to go?

So then, is confident ignorance of
the nova's way, "proof through the
night that our flag is still there"
driving on in a breeze? Who knows?

I wonder.

"Oh say, does that star-spangled
banner yet wave"
at intersections where a
silhouette begins to eclipse the
world of protégés and corvettes

at breakneck speeds too fast

for wranglers on their broncos,

mustangs crazed by storm,

at junction streetlights of

impatient and cavalier celebrities

without their escorts, riding

intrepid down Fifth Avenue to

the sea-bringing heights of Malibu?

And at the end of the summit can they

see, "O'er the land of the free

and the home of the brave?"

LAST YEAR MY SISTER DROVE ME UP A MOUNTAIN

Near Riverside, California (or maybe it was closer to Santa Barbara) last year, my sister drove me up a mountain to look at the monks. I was afraid. Such a difference, driving up a mountain, from the flat perpendicular, "No, you go first," Indiana cornfield intersections that I'm used to. The curving, sandy-graveled mountain road demanded so little space. It could have demanded more as far as I was concerned. No shoulder. Sharp curves without railings. And my sister easing along in her Sterling as though it didn't matter at all that there was no way to see who was coming.

I thought about James Dean, an Indiana boy, driving too fast on California roads. Maybe he grew up that same country way of seeing everything at once when there is nothing at all to look at.

Not used to being blinded by possibilities.

We got to the top of the mountain and drove slowly, looking at the monks, with our radio turned down so as not to disturb them with their quiet sandals in their dry garden. Hunching over joy of prayer. Supported by a rock. Looking toward the ocean. In straw hats.

My sister's teeth-baring wave to a friend. All of them believing easily in the overexposed heaven surrounding them.

I was sullen. It was intolerable. This is not the earth.

Indiana, grayed and gluttonous, is the earth. Damp snow-melt days with wet intruding on your skin. Sloppy average khaki-green living out rental contracts in sub-suburban sprawl. And all the fat American cars.

"Show me heaven there." I felt like screaming at the hummingbird and his broad-brimmed work hat. How far away from this sanctuary can your belief survive? And for how long in a jar full of acetone and butterfly wings?

I could have cried.

When we drove down she went faster. And I was even more afraid of all the sunlight I couldn't catch.

Isn't it funny how little we can do for ourselves?

WHISTLING WOMAN

You always had to laugh so hard. I never understood it. And it was only later that I noticed how haunted you were. Fighting, I guess, with quick knives against your throat and fast ideas away from bitten nails. A little too far. A little too hard.

I've never understood why I have to use my best manners in the homes which break the most rules where the meanest adults live. But I did take my shoes off and kept my napkin in my lap. And that was okay. I was fine being respectful of adults until I understood who was doing those things to you. But I never said a word.

Don't! You can't! Get back here! Stop it! Get down from there! Quit! I dare you.

Was it really fun we were having? They call it acting out. Maybe it was resistance. Maybe it was hoping someone would notice the injustices of our child-lives. But everyone was, so who would notice? I just remember whipped cream-smothered laughing and staging a fall from a third-story window. Remember that? That was funny. Wasn't it?

We were just kids, you know. Nothing better to do than to believe what we were told. What we were raised up in. What we saw of our tiny pinhole camera worlds. So I don't know how to remember those awful times. Because they weren't so awful then. They were just our lives—yours and mine—and friends forever doesn't really have to mean anything. They were just our lives. Now they are textbooks and psychology and discussions behind closed doors and fingers pointed with blame and dark walks through hollow selves toward forgiveness. But then those whip-cracks of savagery were good enough for us to call best friends with the peanut butter sandwiches and the new tennis shoes once a year.

Now, after what you've told me, I'm glad to remember back further to this dead working woman in our mother-bones. She knew we'd be along. So she was happy enough. Laughing so hard and whistling so loud without words, without anything for him to really blame her for. Don't tell! Please, just don't say anything. What if he finds out? What if someone finds out? So no words. Just whistling. Just laughing. Just our lives. With so much hard hope. And our entire friendship welling up proud without tears in her whip-whelped-whistling work.

ACOLYTES IN TENNIS SHOES

I was recently given the opportunity to read at a friend's wedding. I approached the pulpit, which was settled nicely behind an arrangement of chrysanthemums, and stood. After the ceremony several people asked, "Were you laughing or crying there?" And the bride has called this morning with the same question.

I really wasn't doing anything. It was just another beautiful moment. Very similar to other days' moments. No need to laugh or cry, necessarily. So I was trying not to trip. I was staring at the base of the microphone, and I was hoping so hard, if God were in the room, that whatever they needed would last.

But then I began to read, and it went well.

For your voice is sweet and your face is beautiful…love is strong as death, jealousy relentless as Sheol. The flash of it is a flash of fire, a flame of the Lord himself. Love no flood can quench, no torrents drown.

And I know her grandfather was there, where they were kneeling, where he had died. And other weddings and other moments were there. Weighing them safely. Tradition. Precedence. And I was glad just to stare at the microphone momentarily and pray for it all.

The two of them kneeling together, too excited and preoccupied with routine ritual to hear anything new in the old words, and the six-foot-six priest, and the altar girls wearing their dirty tennis shoes and their middle school faces, and more than enough of us under the beams willing to witness that Love is strong as Death. And to know it's possible to invite a God who says, periodically, "Set me like a seal on your heart."

DISSATISFACTION

a not-really poem for Dawn and the rest of us

What do I love when I see you beside me—not in any remembered nakedness, not stoking some old flame, but right now—in the football stadium on the way up these concrete stairs?

There's a long way between you and me and the rest of us. And I'm sorry for knead-loving you. Vortex nights get dungeon dark, maze crazed, and I can't believe how lifted and lurched with-you I was, how clouds shook the baby.

Neglected? Who's not? Give me precious seams of history to run my fingers down. Give me something to suck. Give me time.

He's kissing and calling and such easy support. I'm holding him back but pillows can't suffocate the need-nights. And it doesn't matter if I want to rush through you not to plunge, touch, down under him.

Because he's here and he's asking and he's telling me something most comfortable. How can you let me believe any of it?

I guess I could just tell him, "Maybe not," if you weren't so far away.

That's it, isn't it? So don't bother to swell me up temporary whole with your empty undoing and tomorrow promises.

He's watching. He wants me. You don't. He needs me. You don't. He'll move on without me and you won't.

So fine. If I kiss you on your "Can't you give me" lips will you go away? Will you leave me alone tonight and tomorrow? If I lie cruel with you and don't get in the way will you promise not to call ever again from your "I'm late. I'm sorry." world?

And if I die here sadly in your give-me-all-the-naked-again arms will you resign to let me go? And start over, and start over, and start over?

Please?

But, yes, still, fine, yes, I like the stories we told on your back with its thick broad me. And I like your chest with Nothing inside but you.

CIRCADIAN

The sun is always chasing the night. Damned by the regular day. Strange then we wonder why our identities never really feel good enough. All of us children of the sun. If you are there somewhere further than me, blazing, I have nothing to give but the sunset pushing west. And sometimes I think, "Where is it that my midday sun, my bright right-here, real-time sun, is rising?"

LIFE WITH FRAT BOYS

I went to prom last night. Actually it was a fraternity's initiation banquet, and I was the girl who went with the guy who is twenty-eight and not over his keg days. This is not the guy who joked theoretically about wearing Depends to the bar. This is the guy who wore Depends to the bar. Now he works in accounts receivable in Fort Wayne. He likes it.

I spent the two days before in the usual feminine formal dance ritual: eyebrows done, hair done, makeup done, shoes borrowed, dress shown off, body shaved, body ridiculed, and multiple phone calls made.

I loved that dress. It was a midnight-blue column of stretch-floral glitter.

I got ready at a friend's house where our dates would pick us up. According to ritual we did not start to get ready until the dates were supposed to be there. Also in keeping with tradition the dates were twenty minutes late. Doorbell. We let them wait. I answered the door, and my date thrust a bouquet of flowers into my hand saying, "I smell like bleach."

Indeed he did. Apparently he had washed the shirt that afternoon after forgetting about that pack of Big Red gum in the pocket which, "Got all over my shit." He did his best to fix the problem and washed the shirt again with a lot of bleach. Being a man after my own heart there was not enough time to wash a shirt twice and also be expected to dry it before they came to get us. So not only did he smell like bleach but his shirt was soaking, sopping, saturated, silly wet. Everything else perfect: Pants. Coat. Tie. And flowers. But, he stood there as upright and dignified as anyone could possibly be in a freezing cold sopping wet shirt.

Definitely a date of mine.

But who cares?

So my friend and I put on our dresses, collected our compliments, let the jealous roommate take pictures, and headed out into the night.

I was not particularly glad that some faculty members were there as I was showing off my tattoo. There is nothing I like more than putting myself in the position to be judged. I realized almost immediately that my date was reflecting on me. And perhaps not reflecting very well. Fine. If that's how it's going to be, "Jack and ginger ale." Dinner. Speeches. Embarrassing synchronized pledge stuff. Acknowledgments. Etc.

And then the faculty left.

Now, I'm never exactly sure how I really want to present myself in any given situation so I generally choose: *out there*. Needless to say I'm scared to get the pictures back. More than that, I'm scared of what other pictures other people have. (The one with the chair, the one on the table, the one under the hangers, the one—whatever.)

Toward the end of the evening I really was impressed when my date one-handedly held two glasses of beer and drank from one while the other poured into the first. It was a cascading fountain made of plastic cups. He explained that he usually uses six glasses, and I wasn't so impressed anymore.

My date and I, the two oldest people at this dance, took a rather invigorating November swim to culminate the evening. God love formal dresses, because if I had been wearing any clothes I wear all the time I might have thought twice about jumping into the hotel pool. But formal things are easily disposable. I grabbed a pool chair and sat on it, sinking through the air and water, as I jumped. He was right behind me. At this point he informed me that I was not only the hottest date but the coolest date. I wallowed in the oxymoronic paradox without mention but my smile was not genuine and I didn't laugh out loud until he leaned over in the car, almost to nuzzle, and said quiet-carefully, "Hey, you smell like bleach."

INTERNAL STRUGGLE

It is a possession. I am possessed by it. Creation is difficult. I imagine a steel taper, round but drawn out to a sharp point like an icicle. This is inspiration. And then I come naked and try to find a way to meld my body to it. I am round and full of blood. I can wrap myself around the shaft of inspiration but I feel this is not enough. I want to bring myself to the tip. And there it is sharp. Very, very sharp.

I am learning and so perforated by this beautiful thing that my flesh is pricked, bleeding, and scarred. There are holes in my feet from where I tried to climb and I have only just missed being staked clean through.

On the cloudy days when the rod lies before me dull and without its glint I believe I can conquer it.

There is time to learn balance. A few moments more. A few moments I have spent in the place of that spear. Writhing with it. Knowing it to be a weapon, stronghold, and tool.

But there are times when I sit off in one corner
bleeding and raw. Pain is only part of my fear and I stare at it:
that shiny stake trying to wait out my attraction.

I cannot.

I saw a little bald girl yesterday wondering when she will die.

TOO MUCH SUGAR TWANG THAT VOICES SOMETIMES GET CHOKED

She walked in with the confidence of fidelity and found him instead in the arms of a skinny lover.

His eyes were wide and the skinny girl's were formed in familiar hatred. She must have been in this situation before. He stumbled to his feet, caught between the coffee table and a pair of bare ankles. His hands found their way to his back pockets, seeming to retreat as if from a cookie jar. "Kristin, this is…" His voice was feeble.

She would not let this happen. Not in her home. She was not the victim. Her voice came with that too much sugar twang that voices sometimes get in uncomfortable threatened disapproving situations, "Never mind who I am, child." She could not stand to hear her own name with this Kristin skank's. And she could not bear to hear him say her name like this. She loved to hear him say it and hearing it now would break her.

"Never mind who I am, child, call me auntie, cousin, sister—what have you. More likely I'm just a neighbor. Have to check up on this one now and again, making sure he's got three squares and a decent roof over his head."

She was not looking at them. She took the paper bag she had carried in and set it on the small dining table closest to them. She moved quickly to the hall and found the tablecloth. It was of antique lace. The words flowed from nowhere as she she spread the cloth over the smooth veneer until her engagement ring got tangled in the delicate cloth.

The words caught in her throat and tears welled in her eyes, but she fought them off. She took off the rings, as if she had done it a thousand times, and carefully extracted the diamond from the lace. She laid the rings on the counter by the telephone and continued to lay the table.

He saw her in these familiar, almost natural movements, and watched her head turn back toward the rings sitting there.

His eye caught hers for a second, and she forced a smile. He looked away.

Kristin was more concerned with the contents of the bag. "This tablecloth is lovely. Can I help you at all?"

"Well, child, it's not half as lovely as you, I'm sure, but it is a beauty. It was his grandmother's, I believe. She claims she made it. I have more to believe that she fixed it once or twice when it got snagged by a diamond ring." There were tears in her eyes.

Essentials. Only the essentials. Water. Food. Survival. Love is not essential.

With a new charge of strength she went on. "As for the bag. I brought Chinese. I hope you like Chinese food, Kristin."

"Oh, I do."

"Well, good. There's plenty for two, anyway. I thought I might stop by for a bit and keep the poor man company, but as you are seeing to all of that, I'm sure he'll be fine."

Kristin was genuinely pleased with the compliment. She grinned and turned to him for a kiss. He was gone. The water was running in the bathroom. He was probably washing his hands for dinner.

Kristin decided to play hostess in his absence. "Where are you coming home from—I'm sorry. I didn't get your name."

"Names are burdens, child, never mind the name. I've been on a trip to see my sister. She just had a baby. Beautiful baby girl, with sparkling eyes and tiny toes. A beautiful baby girl."

"Do you have any children?" Kristin asked as she set the table.

What a question. She shook her head slowly, and carefully placed the plate on the old lace. Her fingers traced the intricate pattern.

He had heard, and watched her. *What a question.*

He was standing where they put the Christmas tree, right in front of the window. There were probably needles in the carpet still. Light from the sodium street lamp outside glowed as it passed over his features. She knew that glow. Holding his face. And touching him. She could not stop the tears this time. Sparkling eyes.

"I'm so sorry. I'm so sorry."

Kristin laughed and hugged her. "Why are you apologizing? I'm the one who was rude. I never should have asked."

Essentials. Give her the essentials. "Here. Come have a glass of water."

Kristin moved effortlessly around the kitchen. He remained by the window. Large chunks of snow were beginning to fall in the night, and their shadows in the streetlight dappled his face. He slid down onto the couch under their dark weight. Kristin gave him a look of pity for the woman. He pretended not to notice. Instead he picked up the remote control and began fiddling with its buttons, something to concentrate on.

"There now. How's that?"

"Thank you, Kristin." She drank the water, and it replenished her. "Well, thank you again." She stood up and smoothed her skirt. "There's plenty of goodies in the bag to explore. And Kristin, I'm sure you know where the napkins and forks and all are. I don't know if there are any chopsticks left. But I suppose it's for the best. No sense flipping duck sauce all over Grandma's lace." She laughed affectedly. *Stupid. Stupid. Stupid.* She picked up her purse and with resolution, "So. I'll be off."

He rose quickly and banged his shins on the coffee table. "Where will you go?"

She pushed the fuzzy hair out of her face. He could feel that hair. *Sparkling eyes.* He wished he could touch her hair. He probably never would. "Let me walk you out."

"No. No. Don't be foolish. No ice on the steps yet. I'll be fine."

"Where will you go?" He asked again.

Kristin put her hands on her hips. She had found one of the aprons. It hung awkwardly on her skinny frame. "Honey, can't you see she doesn't want to tell you that? Leave her be."

The woman laughed and smiled at the girl. The door closed quietly and he watched her hold the railing and move slowly toward the car. There certainly was ice on the steps.

Kristin cooed, "Come sit down, dear. Let's see what we've got. I'm absolutely famished, and I'm sure you must be starving."

The car backed out of the drive and headed up the street toward her mother's, or church, or the ocean. He didn't know where she was going.

"All right." He decided to play along. But when he turned Kristin was trying on the rings. "What are you doing?" The reply was thoughtful. "She seemed a lot bigger than me, but she must have delicate hands because they just fit. See? Did you see her hands? Or her feet? I'll bet she has little feet too. I wish I had little feet. It's pretty though, isn't it?" She held the hand with the rings out to him.

Her apron. Her rings. "Take those off." His voice was gruff.

"Why do you care so much? She didn't forget them on purpose. She just took them off because they were snagging your beautiful tablecloth." She ran the lace through her fingers. "I'll bet it's from Italy. Or maybe France."

"Just take them off." He cleared his throat and continued with her game, lightheartedly. "Don't you know it's bad luck to wear someone else's…" He did not finish. He should have gone with her to her sister's. *A beautiful baby girl with sparkling eyes and tiny toes.*

"Aren't you going to eat anything, sweetie?" The rings were forgotten on the counter. Thrown where grease spills and detergent gets caught along the rim of the sink.

Looking at the bag, "What is there?" He sat down at the dining table. It was as though they were having a tea party, she playing dress-up, and he with legs too long.

The girl laughed an insipid and controlling laugh. "How should I know? Do I look Chinese?"

Stupid. Stupid. Stupid.

They ate for a while without speaking.

"She looked so lonely." Kristin was mending.

"Who?"

"The woman who brought us the food."

"Oh. I don't know about that." He was aloof.

"But she's married." Kristin said, indicating the rings again. "I don't understand it. I always believed in happily ever after."

"It's harder than you think." She might have gotten to the interstate by now. Would she go north or south? South, to Tennessee. She loved the rocks and the greenery. No, she was upset. She'd set her jaw and go north. Straight up into Canada. He sighed. He really didn't know where she would go. It's harder than you think.

"I suppose it is," Kristin said. "But still, she looked so lonely. I've never seen a married person look that lonely. She looked almost as lonely as you were before I met you. Married people shouldn't be as lonely as that." She took a bite of the meal. She chewed slowly and looked out the window.

Her features were so slight. *Beautiful baby girl.*

She looked back at him, eager with her answer. "Someone needs to love her."

Yes. She would go north. She would go to Minnesota. She said she loved the idea of Minnesota. What was it now? Oh. She loved the idea of frozen smiles. She loved to think about all those wrinkly pink cheeks frozen into smiles under a blanket of snow. She would go to Minnesota in the snow.

Kristin's voice was accusatory. "Did you hear what I said? She needs someone to love her."

"I'm sure someone does, dear."

"She's married after all. Someone must love her. He should tell her now."

He thought: *She's bound to find out. No. Let it be. Wait until she gets to Minnesota.*

But Kristin went on with her musings. "No one loves that woman, even if she is married. I'll bet he's one of those corporate guys who thinks money is the same as love. Probably buys more ties for himself than earrings for her though." She put her feet in his lap. With her head tilted just so, setting off her flirtatious smile, "I'll bet she's never even had her feet rubbed by a man."

But he knew how many hundred times she had. He knew how her pantyhose felt in the palm of his hand, dividing him from her graceful heel. He knew what touch made her giggle and curl her toes. He knew the careful polish on her nails. He knew her. *Sparkling eyes and tiny toes.* What a question.

Kristin was so young. "Still. I think she needs someone to love her. That's what she needs." There was a matchmaking tone in her voice.

He did not look up. These feet were bare. The heel was longer and the toes jutted out straight from the skinny foot. The skin was supple, but the feet were bony. No polish.

He looked into the girl's open eyes. *I love bare feet.* "I suppose she does." He pulled her down onto the floor. She giggled and tossed her head. She whispered in his ear, clinging around his neck. His skin was alive with her touch and his heart filled with reasons to sweat.

The snow was coming down faster. The streetlight was nearly drowned out by their falling rhythm. The blue-gray shadows made a blanket for the skinny girl and her lover.

She let his hands direct her. She let her hair be his screen. She let him be forgiven. And she let him open her eyes.

But his were shut, and smiling, as he thought about his beautiful girl, with sparkling eyes and tiny toes.

SUNDAY MORNING HANGOVER IN A SMOKE-DARKENED CORNER

He has to say something.

"Nice day out," with my refill

and, "What are you doing inside?"

I'm not forced to look up.

But I do

and his smile is distant, hanging

onto the rail and bashfulness against

his leaning. I'm not forced

to respond; but I do.

"Just waiting, I guess."

My giggle is the kind of

necessary fakery we accept

as a girl's graciousness.

This stiff upper lip

Midwest *née* East Coast smile

is a cover for none-of-your-business

and *Who cares anyway?*

I look away. Toward the wall.

But thanks for the coffee

and for being here with your

inside perfect windows

setting off

the gorgeous day with their frames.

(I shouldn't have looked away.)

There must be a reason by the wall.

Yes. Here. I flick a sugar packet

to loosen the contents.

He waits and watches me tear into it

carefully, controlled

as expected. But I resent it

and also his suggestion.

Why must sunshine

be relished in the open?

I enjoy it more this way.

Why can't I be

here to enjoy this man

remembering what I ordered
and his smile with a dirty face
or something that maybe
should have gotten shaved,
green eyes and skinny
with jeans skies—regular.
Not a coffee seller, but mine
this morning and I like him
better than the rest,
pouring more inside
with a pleasant intrusion
than with his easy work
he's not forced to do.

EIGHT WEEKS THEY TOLD ME TO CALL HELL

Three days before I left for basic training I could only think of two things: the gas chamber and all those immunization shots. When I expressed this anxiety to my sister she said, "You dread those things now, but when the time comes they won't be what affects you. You are ready for those because you can comprehend them. It will be the things you don't know how to fear that scare you the most."

"Well, say something, Private. Yes, Sergeant. No, Sergeant. Screw you Sergeant." I was shocked. "Did you look me in the eye, Jones? Did you?" Petrified. "PUSH." Thank you: action, at least. If I look at the cement I don't have to look at you. And then—right then—she was with me on the ground, hissing. "Jones, you don't know me. You don't want to know me. You don't even need anything like me in your life, and here I am. You better push, Private. I'm gonna make you hate me so bad you won't know how to scream. Pick your head up. If I ask you a question I expect an answer. Is that understood? You better not look me in the eye, Private. Well?"

"Yes, Sergeant."

"You better speak up, Private."

"Yes, Sergeant."

"Don't you know I'm deaf, Private?"

"Yes, Sergeant."

"RECOVER."

I didn't know what to do.

"God damn it, Jones, you want to make this difficult? I said get up. Too slow. PUSH. RECOVER. PUSH. RECOVER. Do you think you're funny, Private? You better motivate yourself. I said PUSH. RETRIEVE YOUR COVER, Private. Your hat. I said RETRIEVE YOUR COVER, you pathetic piece of civilian trash."

"This is the last cycle were going to use these masks. I know they aren't the greatest. But it's only three minutes in your whole life. You've been in once. So what if your mask doesn't seal? I can't help it. It's not so bad. Just get in there and get through it. You can breathe that stuff for three minutes, Jones. I've seen you. You're tough. It won't kill you. It's only tear gas."

"Why are you so fat, Jones? You better run in place every time you see me. I bet the rest of your mama's kids just starved to death with you around, didn't they? Didn't they, Jones? Pick your feet up. And don't scuff my floor. I bet I know why you're so fat. I bet your daddy used to bring you a cake home every day, didn't he? Are you tired, Private? Oh, well by all means—PUSH. Or was it your boyfriend? Do you miss your boyfriend, Jones? Oh, never mind. No one as fat as you could have a boyfriend. Isn't that right, Jones? You better answer me, Private. Isn't that right? You're too fat to have a man RECOVER. You better stand at parade rest when you're talking to an NCO. Dang, you are ugly. I tell you what, Jones, I'll let you off easy. Wouldn't you like to be let off easy? Are you threatening me, Private? You better avert your eyes. Don't no one of you privates look me in the eye. Is that understood? Get outta here, Wide Load. That's me lettin' you off easy, Jones. But you're Wide Load from now on. And when you hear me say Wide Load you better answer with, 'Yes, Sergeant, moving, Sergeant." And you best hope you are running when I see you.

"My job is to soldierize you, Private. It's that simple."

With his brim on my forehead and his mustache tickling my nose, "Do you know why I joined the army, Private? Do you give two shits, Private? Of course you do. Or don't ya? Well folks, looks like Jonesie here doesn't give a dang about the rest of you. In fact, I believe she has personally asked for all of you to—FRONT—oh, no, not you, Jones. You can stand here with me and watch. Isn't that what you wanted? Didn't you ask to be an individual? Private Jones said, BACK. I'll tell you why I joined the army. Because I was broke, hungry, homeless, and it was raining. GO. I joined the army because they take care of me. I've never been homeless. I've got three hot meals a day, and they pay me to scream at a bunch of 'tards like you all. Aren't they pretty, Jones? Don't you feel special? You look special. In fact, Jones, you look special enough to ride the short bus. FRONT. That's it, isn't it, Jones? You're retarded, aren't you? You're from West Virginia, aren't you, Private? BACK. You're retarded and yet the United States government is willing to hand you a loaded weapon. God help us all. The retards are defending this beautiful country. GO. Dang, I hate to look at 'tards. Get down and push with the rest of them, Private Jones, you retard. FRONT… BACK… GO."

"Are you hitting on me, soldier? You're not? Well it looks like it. You're sitting there with your legs crossed like a whore. Is that what you are, soldier? You better keep both feet on the ground at all times. Is that understood? We don't need a bunch of males that ain't balled nothin' in six weeks being provoked, now do we?"

"Lord have mercy, Jones, get out of my dining facility with that Rhode Island chicken head of hair. I can't stand to look at you while I'm eating. From now on you do not get in that chow line until you have fixed your sorry butt up in the latrine. Do you hear me? You will carry a comb at all times. You will no longer look like a scraggly, dirt-scratchin' Rhode Island chicken. I better see you pushing from this window."

"Pri-vate Jones. So you want to go to the latrine? Don't you think I wanted to use the latrine when I was halfway to Panama? Don't you think I had to piss? Do you think there was anywhere for me to go? No-there-was-not-Pri-vate-Jones. No potty in the air. No potty for me. Lord Almighty, I had my ruck, and hundred twenty-five pounds of parachute strapped in my crotch. Do you think there was any opportunity for me to piss? Why should I give you the opportunity? Seems to me you can hold it as well as I did. And if holding my water for five hours wasn't enough, that punk Carter had to sign some fugly peace treaty, and my ass did not jump into combat. Instead me and my unit came right back here. Do you think that made me happy, Pri-vate Jones? You are right. It did not make me happy. Get back in your foxhole and don't bitch to me again until you know the target order."

"Relax, Jones. You got asthma? Just breathe. We're only jogging. Nice easy morning. Just take what you need."

"You think you're smart, Jones? Well, I've got a retard for you. This is Private Blah. Say hello, dingbat. Private Blah does not know how to fold his underwear, Jones. He turned his socks blue in the laundry, Jones. But he can' t help it, because he's retarded. So I'm leaving it up to you, Jones. Since Private Blah, here, can't take care of himself, I am holding you personally responsible for his hygiene. Is that understood? You better hope he showers, Jones, but if I catch you anywhere near that male latrine every dang-blasted female in this platoon will be smoked into the next week. Is that understood? If there're any gigs in his wall locker it's on you, Jones, because Blah, here, is retarded."

His laughing eyes were bright and the sky was blue. "Flashbacks! That's it, isn't it? You can' t say the sog-silly Soldier's Creed because you are a drugged-up hippie. You're ate up like a soup sandwich because you smoked so much reefer when you was a civilian punk. Isn't that right? I bet you're seeing squirrels in the clouds and fire in the guidon. Isn't that right? There you are trying to spit out my precious creed, and your past life is just sneaking right up to getcha. Every action has an equal and opposite reaction. Don't you see that now? I had my day, don't you worry about that, but you better rectify those flashbacks and know that creed inside and out, Jones. Oh, you think I'm funny, do you? A regular comedian, am I? Well I'm not. I'm a soldier, and, like it or not, so are you. Memorize that creed! Flutter kicks 'til you lock it in."

"You know Larry Bird, Jones? You from Indiana, ain't ya? Well, dang, why the heck don' t you know Larry Bird then? PUSH."

"I better call my insurance agent because apparently a tornado swept through here. Do you call this a wall locker, Jones? It's disgusting. What would your mama say? Do you think your mama would be proud of this? Do you think I should call her and tell her that you're nothing but a worthless slob? What's her number, Jones? I'm going to give her a call. I think she should know about this."

"Oh, did that hurt? Do you wish you had your Kevlar, Jones? Soft caps are a lot lighter, but when you bring that weapon right down on your skull, it does sting, doesn't it? Let me see a tear, Jones. Females are supposed to cry, you know. It's okay. I understand. I know it hurts. Maybe we can go in the office and talk about it over coffee. Wouldn't that be nice? Oh, it would be. Just give me one. You've never felt pain like that, have you, Private? It's the kind of pain that goes straight to the tear ducts, isn't it? Especially in females. Oh, you're pissed off now. Good. Stay that way."

"'Attention to detail; Teamwork's the key.' Soldiers, when you are doing pushups in my presence you better all go down at the same time and you better all come up at the same time. You better work together, 'cause it's your buddy that's going to be the one to save your butt when the crap hits the fan. You better know you can count on him. And if you can't you better square him away. When you go down you all sing like my son's little church choir. 'Attention to Detail.' And when you come up you say, 'Teamwork's the Key.' What's so tough about all that? PUSH!"

LIFE UNDER THE TRAMPOLINE

But maybe I have a self-destructive respect for those things too obscure to be recognized.

I think of my favorite flowers. Not a vase small enough to hold one unless mist or dew in a fallen cloverleaf twist could be such a thing. Pin-prick flowers, white with blue even sigh-stripes painted so whim-bliss-tiny that my eyes blur with concentration. They are so hard to hold in my huge overweight hands. There are pink flowers like this, too, and I vaguely remember a yellow. All hiding easily under the short mown grass. Flat faces up to the sun. Smart enough to avoid it all but never drawing attention. Just reassurance for the poor soul looking too hard. Maybe, though, these beauty-bits are the poor soul's downfall. After looking down and hard and sad and forever he or she sees such minuscule beauty. Such a fleck of blue attraction; then why look up? The poor soul ends up wasting the life bent in the search, never seeing more than what couldn't possibly exist. And always thinking: *How clever that it can be so perfectly something.*

I just wish I didn't have to survive so hard.

DOLLAR STORES

There was a woman in my hometown with a garden full of artificial flowers. They were faded, a wax world of *could-be*s: those terrible colors of sun-bleached blanched plastic that grew and changed with the seasons anyway.

DIVIDED CULTURES

The issue of race is a painfully infected gash in the flesh of our trying-so-hard-to-heal culture. Black and white have almost made a peace that seems only to allow new brown animosities to flourish. I cannot decide where I am amidst it all. Raised in a little white town I do not think that I have the same prejudice as individuals raised in less segregated places. My prejudice is toward the people with prejudice. And who aren't they? So hard to learn about this fissure. So personal. So ugly. So silly and real.

There is an outcropping overlooking the infected gash. The canyon is beautiful in its complexity and enormous expanse. Many gaze at it in awe. At sunset it is breathtaking. Those who travel to its core are intrigued guests of a complex labyrinth. This is the beauty, which comes as acid edges glass.

Racism is water (a torrent, a trickle) and society's flesh is rock. So the flesh is pained, weakened, left perforated and unconnected to itself.

Individuals stand afraid of erosion. Whispering statistics. Backing away from the edge in fear. Cautioning their children with lies.

Groups pack themselves as close as possible to avoid edges which might break away under them.

There have been many well-intentioned fools who have stood on one side of the canyon and imagined life on the other. Well-intentioned for their vision. Fools not for faith, conviction, hope, or belief in justice but for calling the gaping hole nothing but a crack. Stepping out as though their two legs could bridge immensity. Falling hard. Dying hard. And so many wishing they weren't fools. Wishing it could have happened. Wishing they didn't have to die.

But when I was standing with them listening to hopeful and hateful talk of multiculturalism and affirmative action I picked up a fistful of dry sand and let it fall into the space between where we stood and the place we would like to be.

And my handful of sand dropped into the void did not become a bridge solid for passage. My sand did not fill wounded hearts or apologize to those wronged by averted eyes and quiet neglect. My sand drifted nowhere into almost nothing.

Why move enough sand? It would take too long.

Meanwhile, I will not be a fool and take a step into the nothing. And I will not allow myself to be pushed from behind by an overeager half-blind-with-belief throng. And I will feel bad I'm sure. But I will not be persuaded no matter how noble I feel it could be to try. What good will it do to perish for a cause?

Because soon it will happen that they move too close to the water which shifts with unguided malice over the rocks. And by looking too far ahead (seeing calm rippling glass streams instead of the violent white thrash beneath them) to a place not yet lashed together they will succumb.

And I pity them because their voices are so loud and if their hands were as strong there could be cleansing of the sickly wound and sutures made secure by black, white, and brown commonality or laughter and in time a scar would be left solid for us to cross over.

Too solid to be eroded by water and a warning too ugly to be forgotten.

SUICIDE

The oak leaves

are holding on too

tight again.

I suppose to avoid

spinning away into

the nothing they feel

surrounding them.

That unknown of life.

On the tree,

high in the air,

down is so much

closer than up.

So with a broken stem

the choice is made,

or strength weakens,

or whatever,

and the powerless oak leaves—
even the oak leaves—
fall, each on top of
another, as winter ends.

Obscured by new-green spring
You never see how glad
they are not to be,
to be done, not to be
oak leaves falling any more.
Oak leaves grounded together,
glad not to be alone. And oak
leaves only
beginning to realize
they've lost the drunk
nothing to surround them.

BIRD SONGS & OYSTER PEARLS

Beauty is defense. Bird songs, peacock tails, oyster pearls, soldiers' uniforms, executive offices, and emperors' jewels, or these words and her used-to-be music. At least that's what my mother told me. And mothers, defensive or not, are so often right.

So much is said about the Constitution and its various amendments. It seems there are beautiful amendments like diamonds and rubies. But tonight I found what might be fool's gold.

Amendment IX: The enumeration in the Constitution of certain rights, shall not be construed to deny or disparage others retained by the people.

Very shiny. Where is the worth? Is it in the admission that a written document cannot possibly fathom the realm of human experience? Or is it that this strange short sentence undermines the rest of the document by deferring to the people who are writing it? It is beautiful, but if it were a computer program, I don't think it would work.

THE MISSION

What emotional rescue? Saviors are an impossibility. There is too much physical to get across when one looks west toward one's sister. My feet are here on a place cold enough to hate.

And then that place becomes a place six inches in front of my feet and that place turns into the foundation of a house across the street that I'm looking at while I'm with her on the phone.

And that place becomes a backyard and an alley and footsteps and spring and fall and someone wishing for a better car and going the wrong way on a one-way street and across another new state again.

And then that land pulls away faster toward her feet. Toward the ocean. Toward a bigger sky. Toward the west. And here I am, on the phone, with my hand pressing against the cold window, hating her too-far-away-to-reach tears. Again.

DEFINITIVE ARTICLE

I'm looking at a sticky ring of dry soda where a glass was last week. Sweet soft white cat hair is anchored in it and static electricity has caused all the hair to point in the same direction. The mess of my life has gathered itself in imitation of a forgotten feather.

Art, dear art, starts somewhere between the stars and I. And returns again to the past by way of a stranger's eye.

For several years I have been considering the meaning of art. The meaning of art in life. The meaning of art in my life. The meaning of art in culture. The definition of culture through art. The destruction of culture by art. The place of God in art. Art as worship of God. Art as a replacement for God. Art as self-expression. Whether or not art can be self-expression or whether it can only be reflection requiring substantial context. And whether that reflection is self-reflection or reflection of culture. And if it is only reflection of culture, then what is the role of representation and how extensive is the effect of the artist as a filter for culture? And vice versa. On and on. And etcetera.

Art is this incessant day of getting up and beginning again. Art is that crazed wild beast you find wounded in the woods. Shrieking in pain. Violent and angry. Helpless. Dying. And you do not have to choose to help it. It is wise not to help it. There are those people who reach out to the beast with bread or water or a salve for the pain. And some of those people perish. At the same time there are those people who catch the beast from behind and beat it senseless, prostrate. And some of those people think they have done a good thing.

Other people let the thing die, laugh as if they have controlled the pain, and collect remnants of the beast to decorate their offices, ears, and anecdotal histories.

There are some people who sit out of the way, watching. They wait, patiently, until the beast sleeps. And then, only then, do they approach the animal. They study it. Find its strengths. And see what has happened to weaken it. And some of those people, the bravest and perhaps the most crazed, stand ready as the beast wakes.

And when the beast rises in anger those people rise too. They assume the strengths of the beast. They pretend the power. They hope the trick works. And the beast tires in its confusion. The people rest. And again they watch. Soon the beast is cleaning its wounds. And the people, those brave sweet souls, do not smile at the beast. They do not even pretend to understand the pain. Instead they lock eyes with the thing. They see the beast's blood. They feel death imminent and still they stare and inflict upon themselves a comparable wound. The beast has no compassion for those people. And those people may very well die as the beast takes advantage of their weakness.

But for the few who survive and return there can be great things. Because the beast, once it has healed and waited for the human to heal, knows all the best places to lie in the sun. And the beast knows all the soft mossy beds where a nap is required. The beast knows the fish, and the honey, and the meat, and the warmth under the snow. And the human will call these things his or her own only by watching.

And an artist is, perhaps, the dying. The artist is spread out thin close to the ground to catch the dying. Cushioning the leaves' fall. Blessing the fish's grave. Listening to the wind tell the last words of the dry fall corn. This is the artist. Not God but a man of God, blessing the death that will only just precede renewal. Holding the hands of salmon streams bubbling with the turbulence of an exfoliating thousand gasping gills.

And all immortalized. Marked with a tombstone. Poems. Paintings. Music. Sculpture. Sketches. Recording it all. Remembering it all. Forgetting nothing. Abandoning no one.

Add the mama rabbit close to death in the snow. She becomes soil willingly, hearing the artist's somber footsteps passing her grave.

And he walks quietly over them all, then, tamping them down, watching them submit to fate, and nodding over and over in comfort," Yes, you have lived your life. No, I will not forget you. Yes, I will tell them. Yes, I promise to tell them."

So in a way the artist does not suffer. He is the friend who grants the dying wish. He is the messenger from one life to another. He is the caretaker of a being's most precious memory.

The artist is there in the spring too. But no one needs him then when the winds and rain, so drunk and spinning and brawling are knocking each other down with their rent tree trunks and broken branches and walls of huge gale-force reincarnation.

Then the artist is ignored. Life is new and strong and needs no reminding, no validation, no hand to hold through anxious bitter nights of unknowing. Worthless, unnecessary, dismissed and forgotten, he must even take shelter from their gay happenings. But as the spring dies, he is called again.

Summoned. Not by people but by the sky. Spring implores the artist to record those valiant violent nights, the surges of which only one season is capable.

Spring demands, "Tell them how the wind howled at the greatness of Green and how Green smacked him right there in front of all of us. Remember? Fucking hell. So wasted. Do you remember? Then *crack. Bam.* Right in front of me, too."

And the artist always remembers.

And Springtime holds tight and chokes on his laughter remembering The Purple and The Black and so many of Green's stupid jokes. And how they all had so much fun together with The Wet. "Tell them that, sir. Tell them that. They'll listen to you. They have to."

There is a place where you can hear a slough sloshing and breezes bending the grass. Countless plants grow there but nothing is more lush than one tall reed. Green grows only from its own source; not like Black and Rain, neither of which is bound. Theirs is a fatal imprudence where no cause, no choice, might ever be made. Black is so much of this slough's everything: the mud, the water, the tree trunks where they are wet, and of course the night. And Rain? From April until June, Rain resents his inevitable making of Black. Rain exists in self-contempt, unable to stop himself from creating his rival. Both Rain and Black want time with Green.

Green just wants to play.

But Rain loves her, truly. When he falls upon her she shivers, shudders, bounces, and bends. If only Rain could stop time, could keep from slipping down off her fronds and becoming part of Black. He's only with her intense beauty for an instant, never long, never enough time for real passion like she makes with Black.

But Rain isn't a martyr: not a matchmaker either. He cannot figure out how to keep her for himself and wishes, so impossibly, that time could stop in those gravitational moments when he just barely falls onto her supple yielding.

Time never stops.

Black hates to see Green playing with Rain's love. He's serious and gets irritated with their meaning and messing around. Black wants to be the sky so he can push the clouds along to get that falling shower away from her. He doesn't want to be earthbound. So he rises supreme and makes a totalitarian takeover of the night. Black is the sky, ready to hold back the Rain, to dominate everything, even Green. So. There's no color. He loses everything to his consumption and misses her so completely as he pushes Rain away. It is devastating to see none of her brightness, to see only himself extending sky to mud.

She must be there. He can't understand it. She was right there. And there. And there. And over there. She was everywhere for entire days.

While the Black night bides his time, searching, Rain comes back falling for no reason, bouncing off what might or might not be his truest love.

Exhausted from the domination and the search, Black gives up the sky.

So Rain and spring Green arise together, growing bold. Such a love is not sweetness. To envy it is foolish. They are so temporary. There will be none of their constant spring touches in the baking dried-out most concrete parts of summer. But. For a few months, up until June, the Rain makes more and more attempts for her and so makes more and more of the Black.

What choice does Green have when she looks at them both? The Rain is so bashful and Black is so boorish. Here in the wet spring Green is not bashful. She is defiant and charges all eyes, demanding the most loud roaring praise, which Rain's thunderstorm gladly obliges.

Black ignores her as much as he can.

And Green knows he's watching, knows how much he hates the Rain touching her. She pulls no punches, says, "Look at me against that gray-purple Rain cloud." If it's windy, then Green says, "Watch. I'm silver powder one side and then Rain flipped me back over to shiny wet leaves."

Black will not dominate now. He can't risk losing her again. So he lets her punish him with the jealousy he refuses to admit.

Meanwhile Rain is good to Green. And they look good together. Green is perfect against the falling down that Rain makes of fields, tree trunks, and ditches.

But Green isn't just one tall reed standing in a Black and Rain slough. She is ferns near the road and a new forest full of leaves.

Housewife wildflowers beaten to violent purple and black-eyed gold and the white sky after the Rain runs off all suspect wet Green and deep Black of a heedless immoral affair. Even the age-old sky understands and is winking with her burning ember racing clouds. Those others know it's not love but necessity. So Green and Black are young again. So what? They've all shared pride and a terribly tyranny of heart.

And it's not all impassioned fight and flight. Sleek Black shows the lily Green her graceful reflection once a year, and Black ripples when the right breeze lets Green run a forgetful grassy tip along his stream spine. She whispers reminders of her reflected daylight into Black's deepest lack of light. And Black protects her. Not her innocence. Not her life. But he wraps himself, night again, around the place where her growing tall, growing up straight, growing higher, fell over finally. He rests with her there where the same gravity that constantly takes Rain away along that same bent frond. Rain cannot do for her what Black does with his so sure surrounding.

He's always there for her. More than love. More than anything. There forever, for her.

But Black grays into August's concrete, turns dormant land to slippery sloughs, and stops running in such high contrast through tall spring Green's provocative fronds.

Black waits with the colorful rocks, once under finger-deep water, who are feeling abandoned too. Summer, fall, and winter, he knows, or hopes so strong it feels knowing, she will come back to him forever in spring.

HE ASKED ME HOW TO LIGHT UP LOVE

He asked me how to light up love. And I wondered. You mean set it on fire? Burn it? Cast shadows with it? Display it? Catch it in the dark? Look right at it for what it is? Welcome it? Expose it? Guide its way? Find proof of it? Give it contrast? Interrogate it? Warm it? Nurture it to grow? Protect it? Energize it? How do you want me to light up love? And then it was gone. So he said to me instead, who are you, really? And I knew. I am the water for Narcissus.

IN A TURQUOISE TANKTOP

I saw a man. A black man

in a turquoise tanktop, in

a cheap-fence straight up garden

of a clapboard neighborhood.

Well-trained backyards will grow

guarded along anything

by the tracks on a Sunday

morning watch, gone into the city.

Weeds and buckets and tires

screaming messy laugh/cries

and shoes and tipped-over

tricycles rust fatigued

by the weight of too many

children, too fast and furious

inside the fences.

But his perfect backyard

garden, alone and careful

did not just happen

in any neighborhood blur.

Philadelphia came to me today with that choking in the back of your throat. The almost crying that happens when you visit time. I felt weak, needing to sit a moment in George Washington's sunrise/sunset hopeful launch chair.

REACTIONS TO THE BROKEN HEART: A MONTHLY PLANNER

January: What am I to do with this foundation-rib he's blaming me for stealing again? I relive the same repercussive week of apocalyptic beginnings. Living it too hard-aware. How much genesis can a heart endure? And how was it before, when we were one? I cannot remember now what with the new light shining in my eyes and the new creatures in my Eden.

February: Driving fast in a thick storm there are windshield rivers forming over my thoughts of you, riding an old us.

It's dry in my head where you're asking again why I held back my hand from the together forever we could have been.

I don't know.

Dots of rain, stunned from falling, pause a breath, hold tight and take things in, before running on to join the windshield streams. Or they're just swept up quicker than that without a chance alone. Just blown back and off streaking into the sky.

In that moment.

Now see the path of you and me, so close no obstacle fleck of windshield dirt or glass ripples between us. But I hold back my hand, for a moment, savoring me in the years without you.

March: "Sometimes I don't mean what I say," he said to me with reassurance. *How can he think that's true? & Why do I believe it?* Reassuring and holding on but then remembering some words used to be: "I love you."

April: Which flowers were those in that wet-stormed tree? The fighting ones. The abandoned ones. Pink prayer hands with their candles close to black swaying branches. Which flowers were those, babe? They must have had a name. You knew. But I knew better. And then we both were wrong. What is there to pray to? The rains laugh too often, I think. And the pink-white fingers fell. Browned in veiny-torn creases at the muddy feet of a Japanese magnolia tree. But it didn't matter when the wind came: votive light left without question, fluttered away out of those thousand praying candles that weren't lit for us, left a green-shard lawn strewn with torn-open, torn-off, torn-down and away, ripped-up, ruined, pink-white petal-filmy hands.

May: I can hear you. I can hear you laughing. I can feel your laughing when there are times when you should have called or might have thought to have called that were filled with each other. There were times when your eyes might have fallen on my picture or you might have remembered a good time we had together but instead you were cooking dinner or finding the tuning fork or chain saw. It never enters your mind and that is why you're laughing.

June: At home, Marie went on dancing with no one but the ceiling fan. There were two eyes somewhere else about to cry. Or so she thought.

July: Damn. His mother must've been seething mad to look down at the horror in her arms. She must have been. Torn apart, as I am now, and abandoned. Helpless. Left to look on and wonder. Is that the way it was, ma'am? Is that the best love can do?

August: Now don't get the wrong idea about this wind. It wasn't a harsh wind, ever. It was a warm, circular wind—perfect for easing the sun's intensity on your back, or for whooshing your hair into your mouth, but not for throwing sand into your eyes, or making you wish you had worn a jacket. It was the music that turned silences between diffident lovers into a song of crashing waves, which they both understood must be listened to. It was the governess wind that rocks you to sleep in the cradle of your house, and the reassuring wind that reminds you that you are alive—if you are forgotten.

September: It's midnight again and I'm writing a letter for later. For the past week at different moments my eyes have filled with tears. I have taken walks that led me nowhere and have started sentences which in the end meant nothing. When I want to sit down, I make myself stand up and move forward. When I have gone on aimlessly for too long, I rest alone. All because I know how much I will miss you.

October: I didn't know he did it,
but he's gone hunting again
(damned) with his twenty-two.
Leaves crunching through
the woods. Shepherd panting
out his trotting tongue. A summer
goes by and he's back again with some

(dripping) kill. Asking me to slice it,

to cook it up and feed it

to him and the dog

as if I didn't notice the

(wet) carcass, bloody red, was

mine once, my subtle

hope, my expectation.

But it was always fair game.

I suppose I even made it a

(fucking) test. There it is.

It's constant and will be there forever.

So he took the challenge. I was

right. It stood still. An easy target

for the hunter

(ready) with his twenty-two.

November: I planted my bulb garden yesterday. I figured I was not going to waste sixty dollars' worth of bulbs because I was a lazy ass who was always thinking about you. In order to assure that I was not a lazy ass I chose not a sunny warm dry day to plant, but instead, the dreary wet cantankerous weathered yesterday. My neighbor yelled at me twice. About the twenty-degree rain on me. About the coat I wasn't wearing. About the gravel I was planting my garden in. About the fact it was one in the morning. Oh well. I put in an excessive amount of pink tulips. I don't know that I am necessarily a fan of pink tulips, but in they went. And I covered the entire new bed, which has been double dug and has all sorts of good eats for little baby roots in it, with leaves from the back of the house. Then because all these leaves were blowing in the wind I shoveled some of the wet broken-down leaves from the street. People rake their lawns. Put the leaves in the street next to the curb. And the rains come. And the cars park on them and break them down. Perfect mulch. And weight for the dryer leaves. After I was satisfied with that layer I went inside. Then I wondered how many petroleum products were in those leaves from the street on my sixty dollars' worth of bulbs in the ground.

December: It's as if I am not in control. I've got the dark quiet, the refusal. I have a soothing rain. I even have the time. But I can't. Why is that? Because it isn't enough to do it just for me. Life begins in the time and in a mind that won't get sad.

I have a fat deaf cat who sits on her hands all day smelling the carpet. There must be better role models.

MR. BEAT

There's a bassinet

on the window ledge

and Grandma's arms

to away-brush the

snow, Paul. Oh, Paul,

such a story to base

your life on.

And from so far away.

DEW

After the rain

senna leaves

are jewelry farms

and the wind

a migrant worker.

ENDS OF GOOD THINGS

My father retired this year. It was a mixed occasion. My entire life I have known him almost exclusively as the guy who grades papers at the kitchen table all night. When I went to sleep as a child, his shadow shifted across my bedroom door when he got some raisins, marshmallows, or oatmeal cookies.

Students called the house with pathetic excuses for missed exams and my father would listen patiently and continually give second chances. At faculty picnics where it was a little too cold to swim and where we would spit watermelon seeds across the cracked cement basketball courts until some priest yelled at us, my father stood talking. But other days we drove slowly all over any piece of land that St. Joe ever owned, listening for birds and looking skyward. Once Dad woke us all out of a dead sleep and shuffled us into the car. He'd heard an owl in Drexel Woods and insisted we come hear it too.

Hoo-hoo-whooo-ah! He stood there in the night, by the car, in the woods, calling up into the blackness with the rest of us drowsing.

Last year I read in the local newspaper that he was having his annual bird walk at Lake Banet. The entire top half of the front page was dedicated to an interview with my father. One would suppose it was a sizable event. So when he got back that morning, I asked my father how it had gone. He said very well. They had seen a flock of plovers, several sandpipers, a few vireos, a thrush, plenty of geese and ducks, and a few rather notable warblers. He explained about the birds for forty-five minutes. When he seemed to be finished I asked how many people had shown up as a result of such good advertisement by the article. And my father said, "Oh, it was just me for the most part. Another professor stopped by for a while, I guess." After all that no one had come.

So what?

That's us. Our household. Summers, too.

Gen ripped and tore through Chopin, Beethoven, Clementi, Shostakovich, Debussy, Mozart, Bartok, and composers I wasn't ever aware of. Hours of music pouring out summer doors. I heard it, we all heard it, while we played football and baseball and ran through the Iroquois looking for crawdads. Strange the culture we created at 803 Stewart Drive. All around us were the generations of Hoosiers, but Mom and Dad, each from a different city far away, burrowed their way into a life like the crosshatched fields. Trying everything to pass the time. Dad drove all over the state fighting for better education and looking for birds. Mom played the piano, learned to paint, planted an organic garden in the midst of chemically-treated lawns.

They were not hippies. Not by any means. Too prickly, Mom would say. Or even antisocial. Not interested in alcohol or drugs. Religious, perhaps. Dad was born in 1933 and Mom in '39. They were children of the fifties. Conservative, cautious, and upstanding. Straitlaced.

And the rules applied to me. No long hair. No perms. No fingernail polish. No denim skirts. No jean jackets. No dyed hair. No pierced ears. No skirts above the knees. No makeup. And by some tacit law this all meant no sex ever.

But in every other way I was free. Free to do or not to do any and every thing. My sister chose to do her homework. I chose not. She chose to read. I chose not. I chose friends. She chose loneliness. And that was good enough for our differences. In every other way I followed her. I was in summer theater as she had been. I played bassoon when she had played oboe. And although I never really was, I desperately wanted to be studious and well-read. Even now I could read all the books in the world and not ever believe I had read anything more than the funnies compared to her.

For the most part it is always okay to be different. That's what they say, those kindergarten teachers of the world. But there were times, too, when sticking out was unbearable. Sometimes there were no real reasons or at least ones people would dare say. But other times when paychecks were small, Mom would come home and swear and curse and scream about not being Catholic and trying to do her job. We always had meatloaf those nights. Seemed to help. Or Dad would disappear for a nap earlier than usual. Or Gen would lock herself in her room and read. Or I would turn on the TV and drift away into black-and-white Zenith-uncolored worlds for a while.

Now Mom was Mom and there was no changing it. When I said she had no friends, she filled the bathtub with ice and invited the entire town. They all came, too. When everyone else had turkey and family for Christmas the four of us sat alone and ate duck à l'orange, cow's heart, mint lamb, or tongue. If a well-balanced meal meant protein, fruit, and veggies we had cheese, apple pie, and popcorn. There were extravagant shopping sprees at Saks Fifth Avenue the same summer we couldn't possibly afford to water the lawn. And most importantly, when all the sameness of the world seemed forever for my friends and me, my mom would flip it and jostle it and cut it and sprinkle it all over us and we would believe again in fairy dust.

It was always a strength, I thought, the differences. But then came the sickness. Gen's mostly. Then mine. And through both an understanding of what Mom must have been through. And I began to realize where the differences originated. The differences of our family from others. Some came from the disease itself. But these are few. Most are from the adaptation. It is hard to live as the one who went crazy. And finding yourself again can be impossible if you panic. So life is lived slowly and thoroughly. No conventions are accepted until they are proven to be of some value. The opinion of others is a welt numb with age. The true knowledge that life, a conscious life, is more precious than anything is a fact so furious that I have seen myself often inflict it upon others who may or may not have cared to know.

My mother has so many folds. I admire and envy them but am so afraid to attain similar traits, suspecting the strange recesses and edges of their origins. On one hand, a foolish person might think, she was an explorer who brought great treasures of the mind to reality. Patience with oneself in adversity and triumph. Humility without weakness. But these trophies are met with disbelief in our time. And like other pioneers she feels only rejection for her efforts on frontiers.

And though I would love to be a fool, I know that to be insane, even if only for a short time, is no great journey. It is hell. Such that cannot be represented. If we are all accustomed to shimmering mirror waters that slosh one-inch waves quietly against the sun-warmed shore, insanity is that most furious storm which tosses seized seas against the earth with such a destructive force that boulders rain down from the sky as sand through God's hands while the winds sing anguished songs of survival.

So my mother is not a triumphant warrior returned from a victorious battle. She is the small sand shrimp who emerges after the storm happy to have been spared.

No. Perhaps the explorer analogy is more apt and the warrior, too. For it is the explorers who have seen the furies of the sea and the warriors who have seen endless death. Perhaps then nothing can be explained of hell. Words must be understandable and we do not understand storms or war or insanity. And my mother knows this. So for the most part she stays quiet, there in her life, like a soldier home from war sitting in peace and never really believing in it. But never apologizing for having earned it back.

WHITE TRASH GLAM

Can someone please explain to me this latest craze of White Trash Glam? I opened up a new *Cosmo*, my most precious moment of the month, only to be met with what could have been seen at any point in my Rensselaer childhood: a scrawny blond wearing a ripped slip. She stands in a sunburnt lawn of a small ranch house. White siding, blue unhinged shutters, broken blinds, chipped trim, broken door—every indication of personal neglect. On top of it all are remnants of careless barefoot children: two BMX bikes lying in the lawn; one smaller bike with training wheels and tires full of mud (a prologue to drunken days of muddin' in supercharged pickup trucks perhaps). Against the house a toddler's toy and a fine example (carefully chosen by a committee of *Cosmo* designers, no doubt) of that strange household refuse that seems to surround so many smaller lower-middle class homes. A large piece of something yellow. It might be old carpet or a tablecloth, possibly even a uniform of a fireman—the father? It is an example of so many uncompleted or unfulfilled thoughts.

It is a rug which could have been thrown out in a fit of rage: dirty, water-damaged from a leaky roof, pissed on by an untrained dog, or perhaps rescued from a family friend's home improvement project to later line a still-unbuilt tree house.

Minus the model's go-go boots and flawless skin, it is a believable image of wilting life.

But why is it there in *Cosmo*, a fashion magazine supposedly representing the cutting edge of glamour? I think much lies in the fact that it is there. Perhaps it is that magazines such as this pursue not glamour but extremity, so that whether the images portray *haute couture* or destitution they have equal impact on the mainstream readership.

Beyond this I think the images of the photo shoot foretell a huge economic backswing. A definite trend toward the conservative. The glorification of the underdog and failure which fuel the backwoods egos of militias. And a primal call to the senses stimulating the sex appeal of the woman-child. The sex appeal of abuse which is being represented more and more often in extremely acceptable circumstances: movies, magazines, talk shows, etc.

What are we to do? In the same series of magazine photos a blond wanders aimlessly. A country road, farm equipment, railroad tracks, pickups, and a dusty Texas road sign support her in the role of a bored teenager in tight cutoffs. Another photo is black lingerie in a cheap motel. Then black leather fringe and a fully-stocked bar. A crocheted tablecloth and a blue lace shirt.

But who is paying for this look? Who are the buyers of destitution?

It seems white folks have turned on ourselves, attacking groups within our own group. Confused innocence asks, "But having made the pages of *Cosmo* hasn't the poor white country girl arrived?"

No. She has been purchased. In a world of physical labor, slaves were once bought and sold, used and killed. And now in our world of images visual identities—represented symbols—are bought and sold. It might be too extreme to compare slavery to a game of dress-up. No doubt it is. But with intellectual property becoming more and more important and with intangibles gaining on physical commodities the apprehension of identity has taken a different form. And still such apprehension is the destruction of human rights. Because there is something important in living the lives that create who we are. That create what we look like. And it is inappropriate for someone to don the look toward the purpose of insinuating they have lived the life that created the look—that they have known the hard days and impossible-to-endure nights of poverty.

I see a wealthy woman—as haggard by sun and cigarettes as any working-class woman—slide into a beach club chair and order a vodka on the rocks. She wears the dress shown in this month's *Cosmo* and is careful that her two-carat platinum doesn't snag the $480 cap-sleeved cheap chic dress from Moschino.

It is as if in a last-ditch effort to maintain dominance the rich whites say, "We can't all survive." And then draw a line in the sand. Those on this side will be on top. Those on the other side are the same as Indians, Africans, Guatemalans, and Jamaicans have been in the past: toys, games, playthings. Their cultures are breeding grounds for fads and deserve not respect and acceptance but denigrating acquisition.

White girls with henna-painted hands and midriffs. White girls in African tribal dress. White girls carrying Guatemalan bags. White girls with Jamaican wrapped hair braids. And now rich white girls dressing up like poor white girls. Maybe not. Maybe there is no effort to avoid confrontation with 'the other.' But it seems a reinforcement of the deepest rift in U.S. culture. That quiet insistence against equity, that there is an *other*. And that the other is inferior, with some degree of dominance and submission at stake, and like warriors taking scalps a woman in another woman's clothes signifies nothing if not that a conquering has occurred.

I may well be wrong. And hopefully I am wrong. I hope that white girls wearing all sorts of multicultural garb reflects acceptance and integration. I do not wish to support segregation which by my argument seems necessarily part of the case. But somehow the appropriation of images of other cultures without also taking on the responsibility of their meaning does not signify real acceptance, understanding, and integration to me.

Just clothes. Yes. But still bright, bold images. The miscast representation and offering of the rural poor to the minds of upper-class suburbanites. Twice today, living in New Jersey for this internship, I explained where Indiana is to people who make a minimum annual salary of fifty thousand dollars. These are the people who buy the images in *Cosmo* but who have no interest in what created the represented worth.

But these things: Stereotypes. Bigotry. Prejudice. Simplifications. Generalizations. Toxins. The country woman looks at the page as I did today and sees reflected there on page 211 a woman similar to herself yet lifeless—clichéd. If she is not careful she will be satisfied by this image. Even overjoyed by these pretty pictures, for the beauty is certainly there.

But on another day, a harder day, she thinks, "What does she know about any of it? How many people did it take to make her look like that? And how much money did she make trying to look like me?"

There is no resonance. Only echoes from a deep hollow where character, integrity, and self-awareness should exist to make any woman what she is.

But hollowness is nothing to most people. Nothing to worry about. And yet so many housewives realize themselves locked in an image-life, which is constantly enveloping them. And somehow they feel their lives ending. Somehow they know what has been robbed from them. The same as Indians, Africans, Guatemalans, Jamaicans, and even the White Trash Girls before them.

A friend. A red-roses-and-dancing friend met me at a bar full of regulars. Regular clothes. Regular drinks. Regular customers. And their regular conversation. A banker. A lawyer. And an insurance salesman. Living the beginning of every regular joke there. In that red bar. Discussing the regular South Jersey God.

THE PILOT

Can you believe there's

nothing there,

no strings or cables or

fraudulent illusion

attached over, under, and

around the clouds he

has to breathe?

PROPHET'S ROCK

He hushed me, condescending. "They died here." But his silence was the inviting kind, which tries too hard toward something profound. And as we walked toward the end of dusk crossing the September battlefield, I listened to screeching hawks echo each other from sycamore cliffs, warning us of some small gossip.

I looked out through a goldenrod sea and sank into it up to my shoulders looking for buoys of purple aster and letting my eyes float up to the sky for a rest. Clouds as coals of a smoldering sunset—deep gray and cooling.

I did not accept his shadowed voice or believe the scoldings of his words. Because death is everywhere. They have died everywhere. Every footstep takes us through the cemetery of someone's lonely child. And if not a person, then a wolf, muskrat, or sparrow.

Each takes turns. Moving slowly, one by one, on out of life. The only remorse is solitude. Journeying eternity would perhaps not seem so impossible if traveled with a friend. But we die alone. Ashes to ashes. Dust to dust. And the dust piles up. Dunes of used heartbeats and seasons and dreams blanket our quiet acceptance that the earth is passed-on life.

Gravity is that weight of our eyes, our helpless wishing-to-be-guilty eyes, resting accidentally on the rising monument of this great tomb. We hurry by for some reason. Blinding our lives with rush, smog, and schedules as the sun obscures so many stars by day—their distant eternities also so singular and same. Too real and constant a reminder, I guess.

So for me the battlefield is a great reassuring beauty. And the tribute is made not because they died but because they died for the same reason, of the same blows, in the same rotting pain. And whether quiet or with screams damning God, they died under the same coals of a sunset cooling.

And if I hadn't known he was leaving, I might have said, "But they died here."

BEAR BELLS FOR AUGUST

And Genny will go too, just in case, for the company of birds, black flies, and sky. North there, to a summer short-wedged down into an arctic year where the aging Earth gets most dizzy from spinning small circle days. Let him look up and hope. Let an absent hand drift over his old white glacial cap as he tilts back, blinking, to catch sight of one snowy owl or tundra swan.

LOVE NEAR A FIREPLACE IN WINTER

Love was never meant to stand alone. Love is as a season. As dependable as the seasons. As true. As ancient. As natural. As real. Yet as transient. People blind themselves to this.

It is not at all uncommon to hear of relationships disposed of because Love has passed.

But what fools would we be if we ran toward the snowbank screaming that it could not melt in spring? How foolish were our tears if we believed the leaves falling meant death of the trees every year? And how stupid if we ceased to believe in the sun as the earth spin-slants toward night.

But we do insist snowbanks not melt in relationships.

Love could be any season. Love is as much spring or summer bright with new life or drenched in sun as it is fall or winter fraught with released potential and dormant hope. As we are born every day so Love joins us. Then Love is something of the beginning and something of the melting snow and something of the falling leaves and the leaning roll of Mother Earth nodding herself to sleep.

We may last many seasons and cycles of Love but regardless of the repeated reassurances and truths of the fact of Love's return, a relationship is so often disposed when the seasons change. As life changes from one time to the next. As we age. But there will be snow next year the way there was a sun this summer. And it is our responsibility to maintain Love's home—the relationship, the marriage, whatever—while Love is a formless misunderstanding.

No one believes this. They say, "We do not have to work at this. We should not have to. If it is true Love." Strange. Or, "We should not try to do anything; we should just be." I don't know.

Because yes, I can lie on the grass in summer and bask in the sun as I would readily bask in Love. Or I can pile myself in layers of wool and lie down with Love near a fireplace in winter. But time changes. It is naive to just be. The summer child must go inside when the chill comes. She must put on shoes and escape the harsh wind. The winter child must put out the fire and take off the layers as the heat returns in spring.

And that is the work. The work not of pleasing each other by continually overextending ourselves. Not of giving up our precious alone time. Not of indulging each other in comforts beyond those necessary or of surpassing the needs of each other, but of getting up off the grass together. Going inside together. Putting out the fire together. Folding up the sweaters together. This is the work.

So often I said to another or the other has said to me, "Come, it's time. The changes are here. We have to accept them." And between us there's always a fool. Either he or I. One of us insists on staying out on summer grass that piles high with snow around our bare feet. Or one of us insists on keeping the fireplace hot and the wool tight as the heat and humidity return from their travels.

What would you say to a barefoot man in the snow? Or the fire-scorched woman in summer?

"You are crazy." "You're a fool." "What in the hell are you doing?"

Changes come. One person does not inflict them on the other. Who would ever blame the snow on a child? But we do this to our young loves. We do not simply prepare ourselves and our lives for the true changes that come as freely as wind. We stand like blind fools screaming, blaming, refusing, and failing.

Love leaves anyway. And love will return regardless. It is how we wait. It is who we wait with that is the relationship. Changes come.

I am not afraid of the first snow. Are you? I am not even afraid of thick blizzards and blinding drifts. Are you? I know I will survive in my home. I know this as much as I know the sun will rise. Why do we distrust our relationships?

And why when the relationship, as a home for Love, needs maintenance or repair does someone so often slap the tools from my hand? Always with the same words, "Love will survive anyway if it is true love."

I laugh at this. Of course it will. It has no survival. It is the wind and rain and snow and sun and dry air and rising heat. Love will survive. But will we?

Will we survive the changes? If I see a crack here under the window, which was fine in the summer when we needed a little more breeze, when will it be fixed? I begin to fidget, to question and complain. In winter the cold should be kept out. It only makes sense. The breeze will be a wind. And snow packed in the crack will freeze and thaw, freeze and thaw, and could conceivably wreck this house around us.

"No, that's stupid. It doesn't matter."

Are you really that self-destructive? Are you really that blind to what Love and these other emotions can do to us? They can shred us. They can kill us. Don't you understand that?

Already with those last words the crack has grown. The house will fall and each of us, he and I, will wander aimless in our blanched-sight brutal exposure. We will be lost, delirious, and will walk in slow circles around the fallen else.

When the season changes again and Love returns, as always happens, there will be no house. No relationship. No people left sharing it. And Love will sit down there, where that house used to be, looking hopeful, with searching eyes on the horizon, and she will settle down into a quiet grave as she has done before so many times. Because she is gravity, earth, time, and the constant change from life to death and death to life.

Cry if you want. You fool. But she is simple. Love is understandable. It is we who you should worry about. Crying over Love as though her death is a tragedy. No more a tragedy than those houses built without heed to the fault lines beneath them. We know how to build houses that stand through earthquakes but we don't. There is no tragedy then when we cry, except of our own foolishness. Be sure that she is crying for you because she knows and understands that loneliness is far, far worse than any of her stupid deaths.

BURN VICTIM

We talked about each other's armor but tonight I see
you, young child, without flesh, stripped from your dressed-up
world. Every tough painful thing is too close and I know my
kisses will infect you. So I keep my lips away from sore,
pulsing, raw, bleeding, open-sore flesh. You're still here, so
close, sleeping burnt in my arms. But I'm without protection
from your screaming for skin. Why do you insist that I spend
my life getting pretty? Pretty exhausted with a white-toothed
smile. Pretty tomorrow with nothing to say. Pretty much
heartless but surrounded by mirror-skin that leaves the healed
curtains open for the pretty-watch-me day.

ORDERLY

Here I am at the end of a wonderful life. And this is the way I want things. I still look pretty good for my age. Must have been all the years of laughing with my husband. He is doddering around here somewhere and I am enjoying a few minutes of sunlight on the back porch. There is a warbler in the cherry tree and I can almost see all the springs with their warblers passing through.

My husband has just come into the room but seems to have forgotten something and is leaving again. I am smiling at his frail intensity and remembering all the years we've shared as the sun filters onto the lawn.

He's back now. Satisfied by whatever accomplishment he made. There is no evidence of whatever it was, but he kisses me on the top of my head and pats my shoulder with an arthritic hand. And as if any activity might be superior to stillness he moves around behind me and draws the blinds so that the sunlight is no longer with us, blinding.

I would rather have enjoyed the sun—its warmth and emboldened light—for another hour. But it is no matter. He leans on my shoulder and strains to turn on a lamp next to me. It is what he wants me to want. It is the way I will likely want things in an hour when the warmth and boldness of my golden lawn have disappeared into the blue-gray garage shadow.

My husband does not notice sunsets. He cares about what time it is and tends to my evening, as is his habit. He is concentrating and too distracted to take my hand as he offers me nothing in particular but assures that my book, my newspaper, my basket of knitting, the remote for the television, a card from our granddaughter, and my teacup are all within easy reach. They are all here, all the choices I could ever call out for him to come and find.

I stare at the drawn blind, hating the lamplight.

Satisfied with my well-being, he trots off again to busy himself in another room.

ABOUT THE ON IMPULSE SERIES

We each have an impulse to share our experience. These four collections of short works explore storytelling from catharsis to craft. Over the course of this series Nath Jones's writing style develops from the raw, associative, tyrannic rambles of cathartic non-fiction, flash fiction, and rant in *The War is Language* and our digital domains, to the delightful rough-hewn vignettes of *2000 Deciduous Trees*, into the compact characterizations of the fictionalized tellings in *Love & Darts*, and finally toward *Acquainted with Squalor's* fully-crafted short stories that use literary devices and narrative elements to reveal a world well-rendered. In *Radar Road: the Best of On Impulse*, Morgan Sorvillo Kiger gives us a portion to desire.

ABOUT THE AUTHOR

Nath Jones received an MFA in creative writing from Northwestern University where she was a nominee for the Best New American Voices 2010. Her publishing credits include *PANK Magazine*, *There Are No Rules*, *The Battered Suitcase*, and *Sailing World*. Her current e-book series, *On Impulse*, explores the spectrum of narrative from catharsis to craft. She lives and writes in Chicago.

www.ingramcontent.com/pod-product-compliance
Lightning Source LLC
Chambersburg PA
CBHW051652180726
48284CB00006B/1968